The Rebel Christian Publishing

Copyright © 2022 A. Bean

All rights reserved. No part of this publication may be reproduced, distributed, or transmitted in any form or by any means, including photocopying, recording, or other electronic or mechanical methods, without the prior written permission of the publisher, except in the case of brief quotations embodied in critical reviews and certain other noncommercial uses permitted by copyright law. For permission requests, write to the publisher, addressed "Attention: Permissions Coordinator," at the address below.

ISBN: 978195729026-3 (eBook)
Print: 9781957290270

This is a work of fiction. Any references to historical events, real people, or real places are used fictitiously. Names, characters, and places are products of the author's imagination. Inclusion of or reference to any Christian elements or themes are used in a fictitious manner and are not meant to be perceived or interpreted as an act of disrespect against such a wonderful and beautiful belief system.

Cover image provided by Envato Elements
Cover designed by Valicity Elaine

The Rebel Christian Publishing LLC
350 Northern Blvd STE 324 - 1390
Albany, NY 12204-1000

Visit us: http://www.therebelchristian.com/
Email us: rebel@therebelchristian.com

Contents

1 1
2 13
3 22
4 30
5 45
6 54
7 64
8 73
9 82
10 90
11 101
12 111
13 121
14 128
15 136
16 143
17 154
18 170
19 182
20 190
21 201
22 210
23 221
24 236

25	251
26	259
27	266
Finish the series…	274
ACKNOWLEDGEMENTS	275
The Rebel Christian Publishing	276

Series Order:

The Woof Pack

The Beta Rises

The Bite of the Alpha

Other Books by A. Bean

The End of the World Series (End Times Fiction)

Too Young (Children's Fantasy)

The Scribe (Fantasy)

The Living Water (Contemporary Romance)

Never be who they want you to be. And never be who they told you to be. Always be who they never expected you to be.

The Beta Rises

Book II in The Woof Pack Trilogy

By A. Bean

A Rebel Christian Publishing Book

1

Take Aim

I checked my watch as I sat at my desk. Vito wanted to keep me locked in the penthouse, but we knew it would draw suspicion from everyone, so after a week of staying inside, I returned to my apartment and to my work. That was three months ago, when I decided to stay here.

I gave up my career as a veterinarian, considering it was already trashed because of my disappearance—or my running away, according to my father—no one would accept me into their program again. I would be considered 'inconsistent' or a 'risk factor' to future customers. No one wants to hire someone or certify someone who cracks under pressure and runs away, even though that was just a lie my father told to keep me away.

Vito bought me a computer, a phone, and offered to buy

me a television for my place. I hadn't used one in all that time, so I decided against it. My computer is strictly for work, and it's made my life a lot easier. Using worksheets on the computer where I can input formulas and information for calculations made everything faster and simpler.

I checked my watch again as I finished typing in some information. I was supposed to be going to a training session with Logan on my lunch break before Vito got back. Working freely has been easier rather than working under the restrictions in Vito's apartment and mine. With clearance, and my own personal guard now, I can actually leave the building when I please. But I try not to, considering there's a stirring gang war. The only well-kept secret, or at least we hope it's still well-kept, is the fact that I am a 'runaway' here at BT—not actually on the run. If Grizzly didn't know I was here, then we were safe.

Keeping me out of the war was Vito's priority, but it was hard to keep me as a top priority when we weren't sure how much the traitor told Grizzly about BT. We hadn't heard anymore from Grizzly—not that we were expecting to, and there were no more leads on who the traitor could be.

I gathered my things and whistled for T'Challa, who wasn't so small anymore. He was eight weeks when I got him and now he's almost six months old with clear muscle definition, and he's finally barking. Challa came trotting around the corner at my command. He was getting better since I'd been spending more time training him. He was only allowed to Vito's place when I had to be there alone, other than that, Challa stayed at my apartment or he was by my side.

We left Vito's place and headed down to mine. Inside, Hardy was sitting on my couch, watching something on his phone.

"Hardy, you're only supposed to use the key for dire situations," I said, tossing my purse onto the counter.

"This is kind of dire."

I was nearly to my bedroom when I stopped walking. "What is?"

"Your couch." He adjusted on it. "It's the most comfortable one in the entire tower, I swear."

I rolled my eyes and sighed away the sudden fear that was gripping me. "Hardy, go home," I called from my bedroom.

"Why can't I just stay with you? I'm your personal guard, I have to be here all the time anyway."

Hardy's been trying to convince me to let him stay here since he was assigned to me. I won't let him, but it doesn't matter, he spends all his time here now. He's been here so often, I didn't even pay him any attention on two separate occasions when I walked out my bedroom in my underwear. The first time he covered his eyes and screamed, the second time he stared, which made me realize he was there.

I stepped out of the bedroom as I slipped my shirt on over my head. "Hardy, don't you have other things to do?"

"Besides guard you? No. Why?"

I rolled my eyes. Hardy was getting stronger since he joined the training sessions with Logan and me. Bigger shoulders, more muscles, a deeper voice. He was still growing, and so was

Logan. The two had become attached to either side of my hips since we started our sessions.

"Well, then, hurry up," I said as I grabbed a water bottle from the fridge. "I don't want to be late today."

He closed his phone and followed me out of the apartment, down to the basement. There was a fitness center, resistance training wires, training ropes, cardio machines, and other equipment. There were also weights, and a matted section where we did half of our training session. The rest of the session was finished in the boxing ring. Logan had been fighting all his life, he had a rough upbringing. He's been teaching us how to fight but with boxing gloves.

No one goes easy, not even on me. Fighting guys that are bigger and stronger than me gives me a training advantage, it makes me work harder.

Today's training wasn't based on physicality. Today we were doing gun training. Off to the side of the basement was a closed-off room with dummies, targets, and objects to practice shooting. Thanks to Logan, he convinced Vito to install moving targets for us to practice shooting at. Some moved on an interval, others moved at random. It's extensive training but seeing as I've been doing it for three months every day except Sundays, I've gotten stronger, and more accurate.

"You guys are on time today," Logan teased.

"You're annoying," Hardy said, pushing Logan. The two chuckled as Logan grabbed two weapons from a rack against the wall.

"Ana, I want you using a pistol today. Your sniper training

is getting really good."

"Thanks," I said, taking the pistol.

"Hardy, I actually want you to spar today."

"Why?"

"Because you're Iyana's guard. You've got to be able to take this weapon from me, no matter where it's at on my person. Iyana, just focus on shooting for now. Got it?"

I nodded as Hardy sighed loudly and followed Logan to the sparring room.

I didn't take any equipment with me today. No headphones, no shades, I didn't think I'd have those luxuries if I ever had to shoot a gun.

I raised the gun and took aim, squeezing the handle tightly. I swallowed. I'd been hesitant about shooting because I didn't know if it was right to prepare myself to take someone's life.

Despite being part of this gang now, I thought I should limit just how involved I was. Choosing to stay here and help run Vito's illegal businesses was probably a bad choice. But I just wasn't sure what else to do, where else to go. Because even though I lived alone, it was never made public that I was no longer missing. So, showing up for a job interview might draw too much attention to BT and their clients.

I sighed, lowering the gun and placing it back on the rack so I could leave. I'd wanted to train so badly, to face my fears and shoot a gun without thinking about taking a life, but I couldn't. I'd only gotten good at sniping because Logan said they hardly used them, and when they did, it was mostly for taking out tires and slowing down moving objects. Vito was a personal guy, he liked to look his victims in the eyes when he killed them, so BT wasn't into sneak attacks.

I rushed up the stairs to the first floor where Katerina sat at the front desk. She swiveled in her chair to face me and gave me a welcoming smile. "How's the training going, Ana?"

"I'm still having trouble, Kat. I still can't get myself to shoot with a handgun."

"You haven't shot it—not even once?" She brushed a blonde hair behind her ear, and I shrugged.

"I've shot it, but I can't get comfortable with it."

"You scared to kill? Because that's what this business is about."

"But does it have to be?"

She set her pen down and stood from the desk. "Leo, watch the desk," she called to the guard standing by. He nodded, and she waved me over. "Are you hungry?"

"Not really."

"I'm hungry." She laughed. "Let's grab lunch."

"Outside? You know it's better for me to stay inside," I said. Kat was informed of my situation to keep an eye out downstairs. We couldn't have Gang Grizzly sneaking up on us again, or anyone else we didn't recognize. Security had gotten tighter since Grizzly informed Vito about the traitor. Even Kat was taking precautions with her men and keeping a steady check on who was entering and exiting the building at every entrance, exit, and secret passage.

"We're going to my place. I had something special delivered today." She smiled wide and hooked her arm through mine. I'd only recently befriended Kat about three weeks back. I was nervous about leaving and Hardy was nowhere to be found, so she took me out for the day to run an errand for Vito.

I was the only one free to make a mail delivery that day, and Kat tagged along to keep me safe. She was nicer than she looked, always wearing a dark three-piece suit like the rest of the guards with her hair tied back in a bun so tight it gave *me* a headache. Her smile was kinder than her sharp features would imply. She usually looked like she was one minute from drawing her weapon and shooting someone in the neck.

I sat down on her brown leather couch, as she changed in her bedroom. Somehow, the military had sapped every ounce of girliness from Kat despite her late career as a teacher. She was the woman Jewels told me about, the one who worked the front desk because of her ex-military skills. She was also the woman who was assaulted by a bunch of thugs, but now I doubted everything Jewels told me. I hadn't been back to her place since I found her and Brandon together and learned the truth from Vito. I was learning to do my hair myself, and honestly, I wasn't bad at it.

"Alright," Kat said, stepping out of her room. She was wearing black leggings, and a sleeveless shirt, showing off her strong, lean arms. "I ordered from that ma and pa shop down the street. They sell collard greens, corn bread, and all kinds of soul food. I've been dying to have some." Her words were light and joyful as she rummaged through her bag of food sitting on the counter.

"You ordered soul food?" I asked, standing from the couch.

She turned around with a piece of cornbread in her mouth, munching shamelessly. "Yes! I love soul food. I just don't get to eat it as much as I'd like."

I picked up the container of collards and looked them over. "You should've told me. I could've made all this myself."

She stopped shoving the rest of her cornbread into her mouth and blinked long lashes at me. "Are you serious?"

"Of course." I shrugged. I'm Black. This is my own culture we're talking about.

She tried to close her mouth around the thick cornbread, shoving it to either side of her mouth to swell her cheeks. I snorted, and we burst into laughter as she tried to scarf down the food.

"It's so good! I can't help it. It's my go-to takeout when I'm cheating on my diet."

"Well, next time let me know." I bumped her shoulder with mine. "I'll cook you whatever you like."

"I'm going to hold you to that!" she shouted.

I laughed and found my way back to the couch.

"You're not having any?"

"Well, I'm just not hungry."

She set her cornbread down. "You're still worried about shooting, aren't you?"

"I'm worried that I'm doing the wrong thing, that's all."

"Protecting yourself is wrong?"

"You don't understand." I covered my face. "Nobody

can."

I heard the bag rustling again, and light steps brought Kat from the dining room to the living room. The leather chair groaned as she sat in it and she said, "We're more alike than you think."

"What do you mean?" I raised my head from my hands to find her forking collards into her mouth.

"Me, you, and Vito—we're all Believers, dragged into this with nowhere to go."

Silence rested between us, and I stared at the cream-colored rug beneath our feet, wondering how she knew, wondering when she found out I was a Believer.

"I must be right then." She chugged some water. "I had to sign for a purchase a few months back. Nothing is allowed in without my signature, and my thorough inspection of the package."

"The Bible," I whispered.

"That's right. Vito had purchased a Bible. I knew it wasn't for him since he already has one."

"But how come it couldn't have been for someone else?"

She shrugged, pouting a thin lip. "It could've been, but you just answered all my suspicions, so I know it's you now."

I exhaled heavily, shaking my head. "So you actually didn't know?"

She shook her head. "Wasn't sure. But now I am."

"Fine." I shrugged. "But then that means you know it's wrong to be here."

"Where could I run to? I wasn't a Christian when I joined

BT. But I had no choice. I'd been found out that I was actually dishonorably discharged, and I was teaching under a fake identity. I told them my things had been lost in a natural disaster."

"So, you were never sexually assaulted?"

She stopped forking her greens and stared into her container.

"I'm sorry, I shouldn't have asked."

"No, it's alright." She looked up, a small smile pursing her lips. "It's what drew me to Christ actually. I'll spare you the details, but the chaos of it all almost made me snap. Thankfully, I encountered Christ, and I've been changed ever since."

"I see."

"BT took me in because it was their brothel that got me in that situation. I was shut down for a while, working quietly at the front desk, until I had to sign for a package and inspect it. It was a Bible and, desperately, I opened it hoping that all I'd heard about it was true. That there was a savior who really took every pain away. I wondered," she paused, looking off at nothing in particular, "was He strong enough to take away my pain? Turns out He was, well, *is*."

She set her container down and marched to her room, returning with a Bible in her hands as she sat beside me on the couch. It was black and used, colorful highlighters, bright ink, girly handwritten notes and stick notes. I guess there was still a little part of Kat that was feminine.

"I still cling to the first scripture I ever read. It was like God pointed me to this scripture in my desperation. I wanted nothing more than to get out of here, but I had nowhere to go, nowhere to run. I was hopeless. As I thumbed the pages, I wondered if God was real, how could He let this happen to me?" A tear rushed down her cheek, but she wiped at it quickly. "And suddenly, I stopped aimlessly turning the pages, flipping past big sections of text. It was like God answered me." She flipped through the Bible and stopped in Psalms and pointed to chapter forty, verse two.

"He drew me up from the pit of destruction, out of the miry bog, and set my feet upon a rock, making my steps secure." She nodded, as if she was explaining this all to herself once again.

"God will rescue us, Iyana. We just have to trust Him. We have to believe that He's going to set our feet on the rock of Christ and make our steps secure. As long as we don't give up hope, we'll be okay."

"But, is it alright to aid in this wrongdoing?" I asked with a shaky voice. I was afraid to feel relieved, afraid to believe that I wasn't actually hopeless, that I could get out of here.

"It's never alright to do wrong, Iyana. But right now, we are in the pit of destruction with no way out. We have to do what we must in order to get out of here. God sees us, He knows this isn't what we want. He's not going to just leave us here when we want righteousness."

I hiccupped as tears began to flow from me. There was a terrifying feeling of relief washing over me. I didn't know how to be thankful that the wrath of God was not one more worksheet away. I understood now that I needed to do what I had to, and God would rescue me if I truly wanted Him to.

"We can't lean on our own understanding. We can't depend on our own knowledge," she encouraged. "But we can trust that if God rescued the Israelites from Haman, the Egyptians, and everyone else who came after them, then He'll rescue us if we believe."

2

Women

"Wake up, Hardy. Wake up!"

I inhaled deeply before opening my eyes to squint at the sun.

"Hardy, get up. You have to go before they catch you here."

"They who?" I adjusted on the bed to see her. The blankets were barely covering her, allowing her golden skin to be toasted by the morning sun.

"Vito probably wouldn't like it. Neither would Brandon."

"Screw Brandon, and Vito's got bigger problems to worry about. Besides," I leaned over and kissed her, "no one's going to know."

"And if Brandon walks through that door right now, then what?"

I smirked, trying to conceal the joy it would bring me for Brandon to catch me in bed with his precious jewel. I sat up on my elbow and gazed at her. Soft pink lips, honey smooth skin, and a mess of curls were all over the bed.

"I don't know why you're so worried," I said as I roved a hand over her thigh. "We haven't been caught in all this time. I don't even know why we sneak around. There's nothing to hide. We love each other, this is what people do when they're in love."

Jewels bit her lip, the dull pink paled for a moment before she released her lip to sigh. Her eyes were distant as she looked everywhere but at me.

"You love me, don't you, Jewels?"

She snapped her vision towards me, a look of worry on her face. "Of course, Hardy, I love you so much." But the look of worry didn't leave her eyes.

Pushing off my elbow, I shifted to hover over her beneath the blankets. "Then tell me what's wrong." I reached for her hand and brought it to my lips to kiss it. "Tell me what's wrong and I'll fix it. I promise I will."

"I just..." She glanced off.

My eyes drifted down her long neck, peppered with kisses and bite marks I'd given her. Jewels was the most beautiful woman I'd ever seen. Skin that glowed like a thousand diamonds, a figure that drowned you in a feeling you'd become addicted to, and a face as alluring as her body. Jewels was undoubtedly named correctly. You usually found a diamond in the rough, and it would shine and glint through all the dirt on it. But Jewels was like finding a haul of diamonds. All shining together through the darkness and grime of Bellen Tupp, shining so brightly you couldn't look away.

"Hardy?" Her voice pulled my attention back from my thoughts.

"Yeah?"

"Were you even listening?" She was frowning now. I didn't like when she frowned, I never wanted her to frown with me.

"Kind of." I chuckled. "I got lost in my thoughts just looking at you."

"Hardy, this is serious," she said, wrapping her arms around my neck.

"I know. I'm sorry. Can you tell me again?"

"I'm worried that Brandon will try to hurt you if he finds out about us. That's all."

"Why do you even still see the guy? He's a total jerk to you, and you're always on his arm. Do you know how that makes me feel? Knowing that you're here, being used by him. He doesn't care about you, Jewels, not like how I do."

She sighed, dropping her hands to the bed. "Hardy, you don't understand everything, alright?"

"Help me, then."

"It's not for you to know. Now it's time for you to get out of here."

I leaned down and kissed her as passionately as I could. It earned me a groan from her before I pulled away. "You sure you want me to leave?"

She chewed her lip with a smirk, then glanced over at the

clock and then back at me. "Make it quick."

--- B⟁ ---

"Morning, Jay. Morning, Willis." I nodded at the guards standing outside Iyana's door. They nodded, and allowed me in. Stepping inside, I found Iyana standing in her robe at the kitchen counter.

"You're late." She squinted. "Where were you?"

I threw a hand and headed for her couch. "I slept in since I knew we weren't needed this morning with Vito's delayed flight and all."

She rolled her eyes. "You're still my guard. You still have to be here on time." She shook her head and crossed the floor to her bedroom.

"Don't be so bossy," I hissed over my shoulder. "It's not like you're even ready to go."

"Whatever, Hardy," she snapped back at me.

Iyana and I usually argued, but it was always over stupid stuff. I didn't mind it. She was like an older sister to me, and I was her protective little brother. I wondered if she thought of me like a brother, but I was afraid of the answer, so I didn't ask. I stretched out on the couch, placing a hand behind my head. I got comfortable since Iyana always took forever to get ready.

"Hardy, get up," Iyana pestered.

I groaned as I floated back into consciousness. "What?" I asked as I sat up off the couch. "What time is it?" I must have dozed off.

"Vito's plane just landed but I don't know which shirt to wear." She held her two options out to me.

"You did not wake me up to pick out a shirt. Are you serious? Pick whichever and let's go." I dropped my feet to the floor and rested my elbows on my knees.

"Come on, Hardy," she whined, "this is important to me."

"Don't you have any girlfriends you can ask?"

"Well, Kat's not really into this kind of stuff, and…" she trailed off.

"And Jewels? You two still haven't made up?"

She sighed, lowering her blouses and squished beside me on the sofa.

"I just don't think there's much I need to say to her."

"You liked Brandon?"

"I trusted him a little more than I should have."

"I see."

Iyana stood to her feet and left for her bedroom.

"Ana," I called.

She stopped at the hallway and glanced back at me.

"The yellow. It makes it less obvious."

She scowled and marched back to the couch. "Makes what less obvious?"

I grunted as I looked her over. Iyana was a doll, one you'd want to protect but dirty thoughts always made their way into your head when your eyes dropped from her sweet face to her womanly figure.

"You clearly like Vito. I don't think he knows it, but if you wear that tight pink top with those jugs, he's going to know."

She threw her arms over her chest, holding a shirt in each hand. "What is wrong with you, Hardy!" She whirled away, and I chuckled to myself, following her to her bedroom and leaning against the doorframe.

"You didn't deny you liked Vito."

"Vito's my boss, and he's given me a place to stay." She crossed the room and stuffed her pink shirt into a drawer.

"So, you're just using him?"

"No! I just," she exhaled, "I don't know how I feel about him, alright? It's complicated with everything else going on, I don't have time for things like this."

"But you do like him? You just don't have time for a relationship which is weird because you totally do."

"Hardy!" she snapped.

I flung my hands up defensively before folding them across my chest. "Alright," I said, "you tell me the truth about your feelings, and I'll tell you about my feelings."

She stopped walking and lifted a brow. "Your feelings? For whom?" She stepped forward, almost smiling.

"Not until you tell me yours."

"Oh, come on, Hardy. We're not kids. Just tell me."

I shook my head. Iyana and I spent a lot of time together, and since she wasn't involved with Jewels, I figured I could talk to her about her. The worried look she gave me, the distant eyes, Jewels has been different since Brandon and I fought. I just don't know why.

"Fine, alright, I think I might like him. But it's just a *maybe*."

She shrugged dramatically. "I can't tell if it's appreciation some days, or if it's because I've never really been in a relationship."

"Hold on, aren't you like twenty-six?"

"So what?" She placed her hands on her hips.

Pushing off the door post, I shrugged. "I just thought someone at that age would have more experience."

She tossed her yellow shirt at me, and I burst into laughter. "I don't know, I lost an interest in dating a long time ago."

"Why?" I walked over to sit on the fuzzy, ocean-blue bed.

She sat beside me. "People didn't really like me. So, I just stopped trying to find a boyfriend, and I prayed God would send me someone."

"I've never prayed before."

She looked up. "You should try sometime; it'll do you some good."

"Maybe," I said. "Get dressed already. Vito's going to be here soon, and you'll still be down here shirtless." I leaned down and caressed her cheek. "And earringless." Her wide eyes blinked at my touch. She didn't shiver away, she let me stroke her cheek. When I pulled my hand away, she caught it.

"What's going on, Hardy?"

"You mean my feelings? I just said that to get you—"

"You're lying," she said quickly. "You've never touched me, let alone like that. You're not yourself today."

"That's probably why Vito likes you so much. You're intuitive. You can tell things just by looking at a person."

"It's not me." She shrugged. "It's God."

"I don't know," I said, "but I guess if you're interested, I'll tell you."

She hopped from the bed and grabbed her shirt, then headed to the bathroom. "Go ahead, I'm listening."

"I've been seeing Jewels again and, lately, things have been off between us."

"You're seeing Jewels again? Why?"

"I don't know, Ana, she's special somehow. Like I just can't get enough of her."

"Are you two sleeping together?" She stepped out of the bathroom in the yellow shirt, and I smiled.

"Yellow is your color. You look good, Iyana."

She lifted only one side of her mouth as she grabbed a pair of shoes from her closet. "If you want to know what's wrong with her," she said over her shoulder, "then talk to her with your clothes on. If she still lies, then stop seeing her altogether. You shouldn't be sleeping with her."

"I need her, Iyana, and I want to protect her. Brandon's no good for her." I glowered. "He's no good for anybody."

"Maybe not." She came over to me and grabbed my hands. "But you can protect her from a distance and with your clothes on."

I shook my head. "I thought you'd understand."

Pulling my hands from hers, I got off her bed to head for the door, but she stopped me with a tug on my shirt. "I understand you more than you know. Trying to protect someone from bad things is never easy. But sometimes the best way to protect someone is to stay far away from them."

I stared out her door into the hall, wondering if she was

right. Wondering if I was strong enough or if I loved Jewels enough to let her go. I felt her grip ease off my shirt, and she came and stood beside me.

"I left my family behind. I left everything I knew and loved to stay here, because it's easier to protect them from here."

She left her room, and without a word, I followed behind her.

3

The Return of the Lone Wolf

Vito was held up in traffic, so I decided to get a little work done before he returned. Scrolling through the accounts, I clicked on a double-starred account to pull up its information. Double stars meant they'd missed two or more payments on their plan, and it was time for Vito to meet with them. Clicking through, I read the name aloud to myself, trying to remember where I'd heard that name before. It was important, mentioned in passing but for good reason.

"The Morenos," I whispered.

I grabbed a pink sticky note and jotted down their missed payments. Their records dated back to before Vito joined BT. But it wasn't until two years ago that their payments became inconsistent. Eventually, five weeks ago, they just stopped paying altogether.

I squinted at the data, moving through their files; they didn't like Vito and only made payments to BT through Brandon. I jotted that down too and set my pen down.

"Something feels off about their payments." Closing their spreadsheet, I started opening every client spreadsheet with double stars to look over their records.

Most days, I didn't look over the double-starred clients since Vito said he'd caught up with most of them and reworked their payment plans himself. I also didn't have access to all the data until now, so I doubt Vito's been checking over these accounts like he should.

I pulled back up the Moreno's account, but they didn't have a new payment schedule. "What is going on?" I whispered.

"Iyana!" Hardy's bright voice called me from my screen.

I peeked over my pile of files to see him waving.

"He's here! I just heard the elevator."

I closed my files and shot to my feet, running out of my office—but not before I locked the door. Those records felt off, but I wanted to look over them first before anyone else.

I stashed the reports in the back of my head and strutted to the couch where Hardy and Logan sat.

"You excited?" Logan teased.

I rolled my eyes and fiddled with my hands. I was nervous to see Vito again, it'd only been a week, but it seemed like he'd been gone forever. The doorknob turned and I inhaled, bracing myself.

In stepped Brandon, dragging a large suitcase behind

himself.

"Aww!" Logan complained. "It's you. Where's Vito?"

Brandon rolled the suitcase a little further and stopped. "Really?"

"No one cares to see you." Logan laughed. "We were waiting for Vito. Well…" He glanced over at me and back at Brandon. "We were waiting to see their reactions to each other."

Brandon looked over at me, I'm pretty sure he hadn't noticed me until then. Dark eyes looked exhausted, but his face came alive with anger at just one look in my direction.

Brandon had only come to hate me even more since I had no information about the Abletons. He was never kind to me anymore, always picked a problem with me, and only spoke to me to tell me to do something if he didn't feel like arguing with me. It was tiring day in and day out dealing with his undeserved hostility.

I looked off from his tired gaze and crossed my hands in front of me. Brandon tsked and looked back at Logan and then Hardy. "Is this some kind of joke? You guys know there's a rat, right? And you're waiting around trying to gauge someone's reaction when they see her?"

"I have a name," I snapped. "And you're going to use it when you refer to me." I walked around the sunken living room. I'd reached my boiling point with Brandon, and every fiber of my being was burning with anger.

"I don't have time for this. I don't even know why he keeps you around," Brandon sneered.

"I don't know why that bothers you. You're not even here enough for my presence to annoy you. And when you are here, you pick arguments with me or totally ignore me. So the one with the problem is you, Brandon." I huffed, dropping my shoulders. I felt relieved, but it was briefly lived. Brandon threw his suitcase down and marched up to me, closing the space between us in one long stride.

"Hey," Hardy said, getting between us. "That's enough, Brandon."

"Piss off, little boy, this has nothing to do with you," Brandon said hotly.

"Back off," Hardy said loudly.

"You want to repeat this again?" Brandon threatened. I remembered the last time they got into a fight, he nearly knocked Hardy out. "I guess I should break something this time," Brandon growled, but Hardy wasn't scared.

He lifted his chin and smiled. "Whenever you're ready."

"Hardy," I called, "that's enough."

Hardy lifted a hand. "Hold on, Iyana, Brandon's always walking around with a stick up his—"

"Alright," Logan stood finally, "both of you back up. No one's fighting today."

Brandon stepped back and shot his eyes up and down Logan's frame. Logan didn't move. He shifted his weight from one foot to the other before running a hand through his dark hair.

"Who do you think you're talking to?" Brandon stepped from Hardy to Logan, his silk black shirt shifting against his broad chest.

"Brandon, come on." Logan chuckled. "You don't want to do this."

"No, *you* don't want to do this."

"What is going on?" We all snapped our attention to the front door.

It was Vito. He was standing in a grey sweatshirt with the word BAPE written across it, and the signature shark shorts. One leg was black and the other was camouflage with sharks on each side. He glanced around the room, dark brows lowered, his mouth pulled into a tight frown.

"I'm exhausted. I leave to make sure our place is good, and I come back to you idiots still having a pissing contest! Brandon, you're going to have to get some anger management," he said hotly. "And, Hardy, stop trying to challenge Brandon. Logan," he sneered, "I leave you in charge when I'm gone, so I expect to come back to no problems."

"Sorry, boss." Logan dropped his head.

"What about her?" Brandon pointed at me. "You've got nothing to say to her?"

Vito eyed me, and then looked back at Brandon. "Should I?"

"Yes?" Brandon made a face like something awful and tossed his hands up. "You're always protecting her. You get so weak around her."

Vito ripped a gun from his waistband and crossed the room in a flash to shove his gun in Brandon's face. "I said I'm exhausted," Vito said quietly. "Which means I don't want to hear about nonsense or how you feel about me. The next person to open their mouth is getting their brains blown out."

Brandon was stunned, and so were the rest of us.

Vito lowered his gun and turned to walk away.

"Yeah, you must be tired to wave a gun in my face. Especially after I—"

Vito whirled around and shot the floor by Brandon's feet. He hiked his knees up to jump away. I screamed and covered my ears while Hardy and Logan only stared.

"I just said the next person who opens their mouth is getting their brains blown out. You're not an exception to my rules, Brandon. Because what you do for BT," he stepped towards him, "it benefits you even more than me. So don't talk to me about what you're doing." Vito turned to head to his bedroom. "Everybody get out. I want to be alone." He crossed into the hall and disappeared.

Brandon walked out and slammed the door shut.

Hardy sighed. "Let's go, Iyana."

"You go ahead," I said as I turned to head to Vito's room.

"Iyana, don't," Logan called. "He just *shot* at Brandon. The trip didn't go well, just leave him to figure it out."

"He needs help." I stopped in the hall and placed a hand on the wall beside me. "He's never this angry."

Without another word, I left them in the living room and made my way down the wide hall to Vito's bedroom. Nervously, I raised a fist to knock, but noticed the door wasn't shut all the way. I took a deep breath and grabbed the handle to push the door open.

"Vito?"

"I said go home!" he hollered.

I jumped in the doorway, trembling at his piercing yell. It was the cry of that lone wolf again. The one that wanted help, but also wanted to keep everyone at bay in case an enemy was nearby.

"Vito," I whispered. I couldn't get myself to say anything else. Leaning down, I took my heels off, and pulled the door closed. Tiptoeing by his bed, I found him sitting on the other side of it with his Bible open.

"News is out that Grizzly came to visit me. If I don't keep Grizzly in check and find that rat, a major client will leave."

"Vito, we'll find—"

"I need to find him *now*!" He slammed his fist down. I jumped at the thump, I'd never seen Vito so hurt, so desperate. I swallowed thickly, and slowly lowered myself beside him.

"And," I whispered as a tear rolled down my cheek, "call on me in the day of trouble. I will deliver you, and you will honor me. That was the scripture I recited to myself every day when I got here. It comes from the book of Psalms, chapter fifty, verse fifteen. It was the only scripture I could remember about God rescuing me." I chuckled, wiping at my tear. "I thought that God had forsaken me, and I was being punished. But then, I started trying to see the situation differently. I thought maybe something good could come from this."

"What good could come from losing everything?"

Silence hovered over us, settling like a thick layer of dust on our shoulders.

"Someone once asked, could anything good come from Nazareth? Could anything good come from death? No one in a million years would've thought that death could bring life. But the death of Jesus brought us life. It was a horrible and brutal death. Jesus gave up everything. If we are no better than the Master, then what do you think will happen to us?"

Vito shook his head, "If I lose everything, what I am supposed to do?"

"You start over. You die to this life and rise to a new one. Vito, Woof Pack is not all that you are."

He took a deep breath and sighed. "Even if this was His plan to get me out of here, I don't want to go down like this."

"Then let God fight this battle for you. Stop trying to figure it out all alone."

I reached for his hand and, gently, I placed mine on top of his. He looked over at me, his eyes wide with fear and uncertainty. "Let me help you figure this out, Vito."

He shook his head. "I can't put you in danger."

"You're not. I'll be alright."

He grunted and looked away. "I'm sorry I yelled at you."

"I was kind of scared." I tried to hide my shaky voice, but he noticed it anyway.

"You're still scared." He looked at me. "I'm sorry, Iyana."

4

The Current in the Water

Twirling my pen through my fingers, I tried to come up with a way to earn the trust of my clients or to bring in new clients. It was hard to think when finding this rat was all I wanted to focus on. It's been three months, and I've gotten nowhere. Unfortunately, most of BT knows about it now since Gang Grizzly made such an entrance in their black trucks and brown fur coats in the middle of the day.

I sighed, turning in my chair. I watched the snow fall silently. Christmas was almost here, and in New York City, it's one of the most remarkable things to see. The busy city was covered in a blanket of fluffy white snow. People huddled together as the temperatures brought us closer. The lights glittered and danced, reflecting off the snow, even the simple red and green traffic lights looked merry and bright.

If it weren't for this rat, I'd be trying to put something together for Iyana's sake. It's her first Christmas away from home, and I wanted to do something nice for her, but I'm not sure if it's right to throw a party in the middle of this chaos, along with Brandon snapping at everyone.

Lately, he's been more petulant than ever. He still hates Hardy, which is understandable, but I thought he'd let it go considering he'd been sleeping with Jewels when I was seeing her, but I digress. He's never been fond of Logan, but that's because Logan's never been afraid of Brandon. But he dislikes him more now since Logan was the one who broke up the fight between him and Hardy. And Iyana, I'm not entirely sure why he's suddenly against her, but if she didn't sleep with him—which I'm certain she didn't—then he's never going to like her.

"Knock, knock," Iyana called as she pushed open my office door. I'd been sulking ever since I screamed at her two days ago. But she's been acting like it never happened, so I try to force awkward smiles, and chummy conversations at meals.

"Morning, Iyana." My eyes dropped to her pink blouse, and I tried hard to ignore the way her clothes clung to her thin frame, especially her white pencil skirt with the split up the side. I dragged my eyes back to hers to find her standing there with a weird look on her face like she was trying to figure out why I was staring so hard.

I cleared my throat loudly. "You get a new outfit?" I was sweating as I leaned back in my chair and tried to act nonchalant.

She stepped further into my office. "It isn't new, I just

haven't worn these clothes yet." She shivered. "It's cold out now, and this blouse is a little warmer than it looks."

I shot her a quick smile before looking back at my black screen as she stood beside my desk. "Vito, I want to go out today."

"Alright." I sat up in my chair and moved my mouse around. "It doesn't look like we have anything special scheduled today, so you're dismissed."

She nodded. "Great. But Hardy is busy right now."

I shrugged. "Then take someone else. You want to go with Logan?" I reached for my phone, but she snapped a loud 'No' at me.

I stood, and she shrank before me. Her upturned eyes were smiling today. I still remembered when they never smiled or did anything more than cry. "What's going on, Iyana?"

She swallowed and lifted a shoulder. She always did that when she wanted something from me. Last time she wanted me to let Kat eat dinner with us, despite how much I liked our private dinners. Before that, she asked me for a study Bible, and before that a special dog food for Challa. She never really wanted anything extravagant, but she always felt the need to cower to ask me for something. I didn't like that she felt that way, but I didn't have time to change her mind about me right now.

"Well," she paused—that was always when Iyana seemed most confident, when she explained why she should be able to ask for whatever she wanted to ask for, and why she needed whatever she was going to ask for. "I just think that sometimes

I deserve to go out and do things."

"You're not going by yourself. That's the only thing you can't do, Iyana."

She nodded. "No, I know. I actually wasn't asking to go alone." I raised a brow, but she surged on anyway. "I wanted to go somewhere with you."

A small gust of wind shot from my nose at her request. It felt like someone slapped my belly instead of punching it, forcing a little air out.

"Me?"

She nodded, her curls bobbing with her.

"Where do you want to go?"

"I want you to come with me to meet someone."

"Who are you meeting outside of this tower?"

I came from around the desk, but she didn't get scared and cower, probably because she was lost in her thoughts, smiling sheepishly at the floor.

"It's my mother," she said. "Logan was out the other day and said the traffic was slowed to let bike riders through. He said they were riding to support Velma Walters. He asked if I knew her, and I told him she was my mother. He did me a favor and did a little research and found she has visiting hours open to the public now." She looked up at me, her eyes filling with mist. "I know she's just a charity case to my father, but at least now it's not just the people my father put on a list who's allowed to visit her. Anyone can."

"Why do you want me to go?"

She stammered for a moment, her mouth opened and

closed twice before she said, "I knew I couldn't go alone, and since I'd already told you about my family, I thought I'd ask if you'd go with me."

"Isn't this private?" I asked, fishing to see if Iyana was letting me into her personal life. It felt like a million decades passed before she said, "It is, but—" that was enough for me.

"Alright. We'll go right now. Go get your coat and boots."

She blinked. "Really?"

"Yeah. It's your mom," I said, "we should go before others show up."

"Right." She turned and walked briskly to the door before stopping. "Vito," she said over her shoulder. I looked at her, and she was wearing a warm smile. "Thank you." She opened the door and left, and I heaved a deep sigh. I didn't know I'd been holding my breath that whole time.

We pulled up to St. Sessa's Hospital and parked in the visitor's lot. I drove today since this was something special, something private. Iyana was letting me in—finally—and I was not going to mess this up. I placed a hand on the small of her back and guided her through the lot and into the main entrance. A woman sitting at a wide red and grey desk flashed a big smile at us. Red painted lips and cheap makeup creased in her crow's feet as she welcomed us inside.

"Welcome to Saint Sessa's Hospital. Are you visiting or admitting someone?"

"Visiting," Iyana said.

The woman nodded and began clicking around on her desk

computer. "And who are you visiting?"

"Velma Walters."

The woman smiled and nodded. "That woman used to get no visitors after her daughter disappeared. Her husband came by when he could, but she usually laid alone in that bed." She sucked her teeth and shook her head, red curls twisting beside her. "Poor lady. But now, the last two weeks, community members have come by even for five minutes just to say hello or drop off flowers and balloons. She's getting so much love now."

Iyana was trembling as she stood there, gripping the counter for support. Without it there, I was certain she'd tip over. I slipped my arm around her waist and pulled her into me. The sudden action made her snap out of her trembling trance and glance up at me.

I nodded at her and said to the woman, "My wife and I just wanted to show support today, hopefully we'll be back. Do you know how much longer it'll take to check us in?"

She waved a pale hand at us and smiled widely, any wider and her eyes would close. "Just need your IDs and then we'll be all set. I know newlyweds have lots of business to take care of." She winked at me, but I held the same smile I'd been holding. Iyana had already been blinking at me, now she looked hopeless.

"Don't worry, dolly," I said to her. "I've got your ID with mine. You left your wallet on the counter this morning, and I grabbed it on my way out." I lifted the fake ID I had made for Iyana a month ago and passed it to the woman. When she started going out more, I was afraid she might need one, so I had it made for a just-in-case situation.

"California? You two aren't from here?"

"No, my wife and I are on a business trip. But our ties run deep here, and we wanted to participate in this… cause."

"Oh my goodness! How kind! Two businesspeople taking time to do something like this, y'all employees must love y'all. Such sweet people. And who better to work with than your spouse, right?"

I looked down at Iyana, and her cheeks were flushed. My chest tightened and I shot my eyes back at the woman at the desk as she returned our IDs to us.

"Alright, Mr. Cortez Ortega and Mrs. Analese Ortega, you're all set. There's no one there right now, so you guys have the room all to yourselves."

I murmured a 'thanks' as I took our IDs and put them away.

When we were clear of everyone, and on the elevator, Iyana turned to me and asked, "When did you get me a fake ID?"

"Not too long ago," I said. "I thought you might need one since you started leaving the tower more often."

"Analese Ortega?" She crossed her arms. "Your wife?"

"Come on…" I leaned down and whispered against her neck. "You were happy about being Mrs. Ortega." I stepped back to make eye contact with her, and there was a dreamy look in her eyes, like she might've enjoyed me whispering against her skin even more than being Mrs. Ortega.

The elevator dinged, and the doors opened. Iyana

swallowed and pushed by me.

"You were happy I pretended to be Mrs. Ortega," she said sassily before leaving the elevator.

I quirked a brow and rushed out before the doors closed. Iyana's never spoken to me like that before. Her words were so sensual, dripping with a purr I've never heard in her voice before. I followed behind her through the halls. Stepping around machines, and monitors on wheels, passing doctors in long coats, and nurses in dark blue scrubs and green scrubs until we made it to the eighth room on the right side.

We stopped in front of the room where a woman lay in bed. She looked like she was sleeping, her hands were still by her side, her chest rising and falling rhythmically.

Iyana pressed a hand to the glass, fighting every gland in her eyes to keep from crying. Her mother didn't look bad, but she did look weak like, somehow, even within her comatose state, she was giving up on waking up.

"She's been alone for so long with no idea why I stopped visiting, or why dad stopped visiting. And now, all these people are pouring in, treating her like a charity case." She shook her head. "Mom never liked a lot of attention; she didn't need everyone's support. I know she hates this." She wiped at her tears.

"Why don't you go in first," I said. "Talk to her. Tell her why you've been missing, and then I'll come in and introduce myself, alright?"

"Okay," she said.

She stepped into the room and stood by her mother's bed.

She didn't say anything for a while, just stood there, looking her mother over.

My phone vibrated, jerking me away from the window. There was a text from Logan.

Call me.

I sent him a quick reply.

No.

Logan: It's important!!

Me: No.

I knew it wasn't important because he hadn't called me. Logan always called when something serious happened or if he needed my permission for something.

Logan: It's about Iyana.

I stared at the phone, and then glanced back at the window. Iyana was still standing there, she hadn't moved or said anything to her mother. I grunted and hit Logan's name to call him. He picked up on the first ring.

"Boss!" he exclaimed.

"I don't—"

"Hey, boss." I recognized the second voice.

"Hardy? What do you guys want?" I snapped into the phone. A nurse carrying a folder jumped when I snapped. I nodded at him and turned to head down the hall.

"Geez, boss, calm down. How's your date with Iyana?"

"I'm in a hospital right now and… wait, how'd you know I was out with Iyana?"

Logan and Hardy laughed loudly before Logan said, "I told her the information about her mother. She said she wanted to go, and I suggested you go with her. She wanted to take you anyway, she just wasn't sure how to ask."

"I told her to wear the pink, it makes her boobs look amazing." Hardy chuckled.

"Shut up, Hardy," I seethed.

"You should be thanking us," Logan said proudly. "We're just trying to help your wrecked loved life."

"My love life is not wrecked, and I don't need help!"

Two ladies eyed me from a desk, and I turned and stepped into the men's bathroom. "Listen," I said hotly, "whatever you guys are telling her, stop it."

"That's just your way of thanking us. Just don't come home without kissing her," Logan teased.

"I have other things to worry about besides kisses, Logan. I'd appreciate it if you and Hardy would both worry about other things as well." I put a hand on the wall, feeling embarrassed and exposed, but secretly thankful. Hardy and Logan had talked Iyana up to asking me to go with her, and I was incredibly grateful.

"Whatever, Vee," Logan said. "I know you're happy, and that's all I want."

"I'm touched," I said flatly. "I have to go."

"So, you're seriously not going to thank us?" Hardy asked.

"You both should be thanking *me* that I haven't returned home and killed you for meddling with my personal life."

I hung up the phone, dropping my shoulders with a loud sigh. It took me a moment to pull it together, but I shook my head and headed back to Mrs. Walters' room. When I arrived,

Iyana was sitting and chatting, I wasn't even sure if she knew I'd ever left.

Taking a deep breath, I stepped into the room. Iyana looked over at me, no tears, no trembling, she was giving me a half smile as I sat beside her.

"How is she?" I asked.

"She's alright, I've seen her better though." Her mother looked strikingly similar to Iyana. Brown skin, big eyes, and full lips, she even shared the same nose as Iyana.

"You guys look just alike."

Iyana laughed lightly and looked back at her mom. "Everyone has always said that."

"It's strange the woman at the front desk didn't recognize you."

She shrugged. "Maybe she's never seen my mother before, just knows who comes in to visit her."

I nodded in agreement.

"Mom," Iyana whispered, "this is Vito, the one I was telling you about. He's the one who's responsible for all of this."

I blinked. "You told her everything?"

"She needs to know the truth. Especially if dad has been lying to her about me."

"I see," I said, looking down at Velma. Iyana released her mother's hand into mine, and said, "She likes for her hand to be held."

"Ok." I adjusted in the seat, wondering where to start. A warmth bloomed in my hand as Iyana interlocked her fingers with my own. I stared at our hands; hers in my left, her mother's in my right. Something felt right, like everything was going to be alright. It was a touch I didn't know I longed for or needed.

Clearing my throat, my eyes landed on her mother again. "I'm sorry, Mrs. Walters. My bad business ended up getting your daughter involved with my gang, Bellen Tupp. But I promise to protect her and get her back home soon. This isn't permanent for her." I paused, thinking over the scripture from Psalms that Iyana had given me. Her encouraging words that ignited a new flame in my heart. I'd succumbed to my circumstances here at BT; resolved to stay until someone killed me or took my place. But Iyana opened my eyes to see that maybe I didn't have to live this life forever, maybe I could leave it all behind someday.

"It's not permanent for me either," I said.

Iyana smiled softly, and I felt my chest tighten.

"But for now," I said back to Velma, "I'm going to protect her while she's at BT. And even after that, I'll still protect her. I promise."

Velma's hand flinched in mine, and I gasped loudly.

"What's wrong?" Iyana asked.

"Her hand," I stared at it. "It flinched."

"What?"

"It just flinched when I told her I promised to protect you."

Iyana was silent, staring at her mother's body. Abruptly, she walked to the other side of the bed and grabbed her other hand. "Mom," her voice came out shakily, "are you still in there?"

Silence. Stillness.

"Mom," Iyana called again in a gut-wrenching sadness. "Please... I need you to let me know you're still in there." She lifted Velma's hand to kiss it. "Please," she begged. "Jesus, let her do something."

Tears ran down her cheeks when Velma's hand flinched again. It ticked for a moment before she slowly tightened her hand around Iyana's to squeeze it.

"Mom!?" Iyana cried.

It was slow, but she squeezed Iyana's hand again.

Iyana snapped her eyes to mine, and I didn't know what to say.

"Say something to her," Iyana pleaded with me.

"Okay, uh," I stammered. "Mrs. Walters, would you forgive me for dragging Iyana into this mess? I never meant to hurt her."

Just when we thought it was a fluke, Velma squeezed my hand.

"Oh my goodness!" Iyana squealed happily. "Mom! You're awake! I'm going to tell the doctors! I've got to tell dad!"

Before Iyana could pull away, Velma was clutching her hand with incredible force. Iyana yelped, and I glanced around to make sure no one was watching.

"Mom, let me go," Iyana called. "Mom, please, I have to tell someone so they can help you!"

But her grip tightened, and Iyana winced.

"Mrs. Walters, please," I begged, "let her…" my words fell short and my mouth fell open. There was a tear streaming down her cheek. She was crying.

"Iyana," I whispered.

She had been trying to pry her mother's fingers off when she looked over at me. Panic and fear all over her face.

"Don't get the doctors. Or your father." I looked back at her mother, and there was a swelling in my chest, an ache. It was the same one I felt when I saw Iyana had cried herself to sleep that time in my office. She had no one and felt alone and scared. I couldn't imagine what Velma was feeling, but I had to do something.

Iyana's voice was fearful, the way it used to be. "What are you talking about?"

"She's crying," I said.

Iyana snapped her vision to her mother, and now there was a river of tears flowing. "Mom," she whispered. "What's going on?"

"Is it the doctors?" I asked, leaning forward. "Is it Mr. Walters?"

Iyana shot me a look, but the next moment my hand was being squeezed tightly by Velma. Silence yawned for what seemed like forever as stiffness fell over the room.

"What is he doing to you?" she shouted.

"*Iyana*," I snapped, "calm down. The doctors will come in."

"They *need* to come in—ouch!" she cried as her mother squeezed her hand tightly again.

"No, something isn't right." I shook my head. "It's the doctors and—"

"Iyana?"

We both turned and found Mr. Walters standing in the doorway. Velma's grip loosened, calling our attention back to her.

"Mom?" Iyana whispered. "Mom?"

Her body began to tremble in the bed and, suddenly, she erupted into a seizure, flopping, and jerking in the hospital bed. Bells and monitors went off. Her heart monitor began to beep at an incredible pace when doctors and nurses rushed in.

"Everyone out! Please!"

"I'm her husband," Mr. Walters said.

"I know, but for now, we need the space. Please step outside," the nurse said, pulling Iyana from her mother.

"Ana." I came over and grabbed her hand. "Let's go."

We pushed past the nurses; Iyana was still sobbing as we stumbled out of the room and down the hall.

"Iyana!" her father called behind us.

"Keep moving," I told her.

She hurried beside me, taking long strides as we reached the elevator.

"Iyana! Wait!"

The doors opened, and we stepped inside. I punched the button until the doors began to close. Mr. Walters rushed at the doors, but they shut before he could catch us.

5

No Good

"He's doing something to her," I said, cradling my knees to my chest. Vito patted my leg and moved to the kitchen.

"Something's going on there, and we have to figure out what."

"Where do we even start?" I asked.

Vito reappeared from the kitchen, carrying two bottles of water and some aspirin. "We start by you getting some rest." He set the bottles down and passed me the aspirin.

"Vito, I can't right now."

"I know." He sat beside me. "That's why I gave you aspirin. It'll help calm you down and then you'll be able to sleep."

"I don't want to sleep!" I threw a bottle across the room, and it crashed to the floor.

Vito sighed beside me and stood to retrieve it. "I'm going to do everything I can to save your mother, Iyana. I don't want you worrying about her."

"She's my mother," I sobbed. "I can't stop worrying about her."

"If you're worrying," Vito said as he set the bottle down on the lampstand beside me, "then you're not thinking. That's why I want you to rest. When you're calm, you can think straight." He squatted in front of me and took my hands. "It's going to be alright. I just need you to give me a little time."

I pulled my hands from his. "Brandon said the same thing, but he was just a liar."

Vito glanced off for a second. When he looked back at me, his eyes no longer held the gentle concern he'd shown before, they were filled with irritation.

"I'm not Brandon. I mean what I say." He pushed off his knees and stood.

"Wait," I called, "I'm sorry. I don't know why I said that; I was just angry."

"Are you going to compare me to Brandon every time you get upset? Because if that's the case, I'm going to walk out that door." He pointed towards it. "I'm nothing like him, Iyana. I know it's hard to trust people in this business, but I promise you, I'm the only one you *can* trust."

He didn't have to say all that because I'd already believed that. I don't know when my mind started to change about Vito, but my heart followed it, and as I stood, my feet finally followed my heart and mind and brought me to him.

"I know you're not like him," I said quietly. "I just have to stop holding on to the past. Old pain still hurts sometimes."

"Only if you let it."

I raised a hand and pressed it to his chest. It was firm, and solid. "I don't want to feel like that anymore. I want new memories. I want to feel something else. Something better than what I've felt in the past."

Vito's eyes studied mine, and he leaned down. "Whatever you want to feel, I can make that happen."

"Please," I begged in a whisper, "make me feel something I won't forget. Something to replace the bad."

Before I knew it, Vito lifted me off my feet. My legs dangled around his waist as my hand rushed through his hair. Carrying me to the couch, he laid me down and I gasped as he kissed me.

His mouth trailed down my neck, intense throbs of passion blooming wherever his lips touched. My entire body felt like it was on fire. I pulled at his shirt, trying to get it off him. He sat up, smirking, and lifted his shirt over his head.

I wanted this; I'd wanted this for so long, despite my caution and flat-out denial. I wanted this more than anything.

But ... this was wrong. I knew it was.

I looked up at Vito as he pulled away from me slightly, sensing my hesitation. My eyes lingered on his figure, taking in every last inch of his scarred, rigid chest and strong abdomen. My hands traced his shirtless body, and I pulled him back to my lips when his hand slipped beneath my shirt.

For a moment, I almost gave in to his touch. The way his

arms around me made me feel secure, and his lips connected to mine made me feel good. But we couldn't do this—no matter how good it felt. Sex wasn't made for us; it was made to connect married people. It was a form of communication that tethered the hearts, minds, and bodies of the married couple, making them become one. It was the drug that made married people addicted to each other forever. Sex is the action of intimacy, and this action wasn't meant for Vito and me to share. Not like this.

"Vito," I whispered. He had unbuttoned my shirt and was finding his way into it. "Vito, we can't…" My weak words grew quiet as Vito suddenly stopped.

Adjusting on the couch, he chuckled and slipped a finger down my neck and beneath the chain around it. "You're wearing this." He stared at the cross he'd bought me to replace my old one. "I'm glad you're wearing this, for a lot of different reasons."

With a sigh, he sat up off of me and palmed the back of his neck. "I'm sorry," he said timidly. "I didn't mean to go so far."

"It's my fault." I reached up to stroke his cheek. "I shouldn't have asked you to make me feel good."

He snorted. "Those are triggering words." He took my hand and kissed the inside of my wrist. My heart fluttered at the gentle gesture, but before I could say anything more, the door to my apartment opened and Hardy and Logan stepped inside.

They blinked at us.

Vito's shirtless body with each of my legs on either side of him, wrapped around his waist. My shirt was open, exposing my bright pink lace bra.

"We're gonna go," Logan said, pushing Hardy back out the door.

"Wait!" Vito shouted. "It's not what it looks like!" He climbed off me and fell to the floor. Scuffling to pick up his shirt, he jogged to the door, but stopped to turn back to me.

I sat up off the couch, pulling my shirt closed and staring at him like he'd lost his mind. It was embarrassing, but we were still two consenting adults, not a pair of raunchy teenagers sneaking away from our parents.

"I'm sorry," he said—then he turned and left without another word.

I sighed, dropping my shoulders. I've never seen Vito so flustered before. I stood to my feet to head to my bedroom when I noticed he'd left his jacket in his rush out of here. I grabbed it to hang in my closet when something fell out his pocket: our ID cards.

"Mr. and Mrs. Ortega," I whispered as I looked at the cards.

I squinted.

"When did Vito even get a picture of me?" I rolled my eyes and shoved the cards back into his pocket, there was an envelope inside. I couldn't help myself; I pulled it out and stared at it. *Where did he get this from?* I wondered. It was one of the small, square envelopes Brandon always gave me to put Vito's stamp on.

I turned over the wrinkled envelope and found the seal was

broken. Someone had already read it. Brandon and Vito's warning washed over me—*the less you know, the better*—suddenly, I wanted to put the envelope back, but I didn't. I couldn't.

Why would Vito have an open envelope on him?

I stared at it, warring with myself not to open it, but I did. I pulled out the slip of paper that explained what was owed. Turning it over in my hand, I saw there was nothing else on it. I sighed, opening the envelope again to place the paper inside when I noticed a name written on the inside flap.

"Renooms," I whispered to myself.

Where have I heard that name before? I thought. It looked familiar, but also not familiar. I'd seen a similar name. I bounced my leg as I sifted through my thoughts until the Holy Spirit whispered to me, *stars.*

"Oh!" I exclaimed. That was one of those starred names on that list of clients who were behind by more than two payments.

"So why this?" I asked myself as I sank onto the couch. "Why them? Why this letter? This letter…" I unfolded the paper and read it again quickly. It said they were only one payment behind and gave a location for them to drop off the next payment.

"That can't be right. They had double-stars. I'd never mess up something like that."

I shot to my feet and ran to my bedroom where I changed into an oversized shirt and my slides. Dashing for the door, I grabbed Vito's jacket on the way out and headed up to his apartment.

Inside, I could hear Vito, Logan, and Hardy laughing with each other. I tossed Vito's jacket to the couch and ran to my office. Once inside, I closed the door quietly and hopped onto my computer.

With my files up, I quickly searched for *Renooms* in my spreadsheets. There was a churning in my stomach, a horrible feeling that I was about to find out something I shouldn't. The spinning wheel on my computer stopped once the information loaded and the message, **No Data Found,** appeared on my screen.

"That can't be right."

I typed in the name again, but the same message appeared. Slamming my hand on the desk, I exhaled loudly. I coaxed myself, "Calm down. Think, Iyana." I paused. "Jesus, help me."

Silence rang out as I stared at the name, Renooms. I pulled up a separate screen from my spreadsheets and looked through the names with a double star. I didn't see Renooms, but I knew the name was familiar.

I stopped scrolling and sat back in my chair. Everything was alphabetized, and when I searched the 'R's' the name wasn't there. I stared at the name, grabbing a pen from my desk so I could jot it down. I worked it, writing it down differently, rearranging the letters until I stopped. I spotted another sticky note that read, The Morenos, and when I reworked Renooms, I gasped.

"The Morenos," I said.

I typed in the name and there it was, the Morenos hadn't

paid in weeks and owed more than two payments. *If they only owed one now, then who's been collecting the money?* Grabbing another sticky note, I jotted down the Morenos again, and went back into my data to find any other accounts that'd been behind in more than three payments. There were only four other accounts: The Stolls, Bozzellis, Hayeses… my hands trembled as I stared at the name, "The Abletons."

My chest began to heave, and my mind numbed.

"These accounts all belonged to Brandon. He's the only one who collects from them. Which means he's been collecting payments from them if they only owe one more."

I covered my mouth, trying not to believe it. I wanted to vomit, but all I could do was dry heave over my waste basket.

Shooting to my feet, I burst out of my office and rushed across the floor and down the hall to Vito's office, but he was gone. His bedroom was empty, the whole place was. *They must've left and I didn't notice.* I ran for the door and ripped it open to come face to face with Brandon.

"What are you in a rush for?" He scowled at me, dropping his gaze to my hand, I clutched the note from the envelope.

"What's this?" He reached for it, but I shoved him, knocking him off balance and running down the hall.

"Help!" I screamed. "Help!" But there were no guards.

I was tackled and slammed hard against the floor. My head felt dizzy as Brandon dragged me back to Vito's placed. I clawed the carpet, and screamed for help, hoping someone was nearby. He let go of my ankles, and I tried to crawl away, but it was no use. He snatched me up and slammed me back down again. An eruption of stars burst into my vision, and my entire body ached as I laid there weak beneath him.

Twisting an arm behind my back, he ripped the note free from my hand. Suddenly, his weight became five times what it was, and I could feel his glaring eyes on the back of my head.

"That's why I hated you so much. You were too smart for your own good."

I screamed once more, before I blacked out.

6

Who Dunnit?

"Iyana," Vito called at her door.

"I've got the key, we can just go in," I said, leaning against the doorframe. Vito rolled his eyes and knocked again. "Iyana, come on, open up."

Logan shifted his weight from one foot to the other and glanced around. "Where are the guards who are usually here?"

"You're right." I stood up straight and glanced over my shoulder. There was nothing but hallway in both directions. "The next shift should've been here by now."

"Something's not right," Vito said, backing away from the door. "Give me your key, Hardy."

I passed it to him, and he unlocked her door.

"Here." He passed the key back but kept one hand on the knob.

"What are you doing?" I asked, but Logan waved a hand at me to be quiet.

Vito pulled his gun from his hip and leaned against the door to listen. I broke into a sweat, nervously pulling my gun from its holster as I realized we could be in danger.

"Boss," Logan patted Vito's shoulder, "let me go in first."

They nodded at each other, and Logan waved me on to follow after him. Shakily, I stepped in front of Vito, as Logan quietly turned the handle. The door opened to reveal a dim apartment. She could be sleeping, but with no guards, a rat, and a gang war on the rise, there was no telling what we'd find in this apartment. Logan stepped inside, aiming his gun straight ahead, but glancing all around. I followed his lead, trying to remember all the things we'd been practicing in our sessions.

"There's been a struggle," Logan said, and took off for the bedroom.

"Iyana!" Vito called as he pushed by me and followed Logan.

I stayed in the foyer before moving to the living room. The couch was knocked out of place, and there were two handguns on the floor. One was across the room, and the other was beneath the couch. The glass coffee table was shattered and flipped over, and there were traces of blood throughout her apartment.

"We've got a body!"

My stomach flipped, and my feet moved before I could register what I'd heard. I burst into the room and found a man lying across the bed.

"There's another in the bathroom. He was stabbed. Looks like this guy was strangled."

I exhaled my nerves and shook my head. "Why here, though?"

"Because of that." Logan pointed to the bedside table across the room. "Its voice activated by Iyana. A scream from her will turn it on and send live footage to my phone and Vito's phone. Only two other guards know about it besides me." He stepped forward and put a hand on the lifeless body. "We sparred together sometimes, he was a good friend of mine," Logan whispered.

"I'm sorry," I said, placing my gun back into its holster. "But the fact that he made it to this room, that's a good thing, right? That means we have some footage."

"No," Vito said as he stepped into the room with Challa on a chain. "It's synced to Iyana's voice. The other two guards have to actually push a button, but he never made it." He turned to Logan and patted his shoulder. "I know it's bad, but we've got to keep moving for now. We've got to find her."

Logan nodded. "Let's get to the first floor, see if there's anything on the cameras for the building."

"Wait," I said, "why don't we check Vito's apartment? For all we know, she could be fine, making dinner preparations."

"We can't waste time like that," Logan stressed, "we need to get to the cameras."

"I think you're both right." Vito rubbed a hand over his thick, dark hair. "Logan, go down and check the cams. Hardy, come with me and we'll leave Challa at my place, and check to see if she's there."

"Understood," Logan said. He jogged out and we followed behind him.

Stepping off the elevator, I stopped. There were no guards again, and deep claw marks in the lush green carpet that went all the way to Vito's door that was hanging open. Challa ripped loose from Vito's hand and ran to the claw marks in the carpet. He began to whimper as he sniffed them.

"She was here," Vito said as we stood over the markings. "Someone took her." He rushed into his apartment and headed for his bedroom. I was bringing Challa to her office when I noticed the lamp was still on, and when I stepped in, so was her computer.

"Vito!" I called as I looked at her files. The timestamps said they were last autosaved over an hour ago.

"Vito, she was here before we left for drinks."

He stared at me, dazed for a moment before coming around her desk to look at her computer. Dark eyes zipped over the information as he scrolled in silence. I looked at the notes on her desk.

"There's some names written down here." I peeled up the sticky note and read them off, "The Morenos, the Stolls, Bozzellis, Hayeses, and the Abletons."

Vito stopped scrolling and flicked his eyes to me, and then to the note in my hand. "Those are all Brandon's accounts." He stood upright and snatched the note from me. I continued looking around the desk and picked up another note.

"This one looks like she was trying to solve some kind of scrambled word, but it turned out to be 'Morenos.' That mean something?"

Vito shook his head and leaned back over to look at the screen. "These accounts are way behind."

"But didn't you just come from the Stolls' factory? They wanted to pull out because of the rat, right?"

"Yeah," he said slowly, "but I took Brandon to convince them to give me more time to find him."

"So, then, maybe they're using that as an excuse to pull out before you find out how far behind they are."

He shook his head again. "No, something isn't right. No one would want to take Iyana because she knew some accounts were far behind. She's got all of my clients and their history. She found something out or knew something about one of these accounts."

"Maybe she knows more about the Abletons than she's been saying, and someone found out."

"Could be," he shrugged. "There's no telling. It could be any of these accounts. These are legendary accounts because they were acquired by my grandfather, but the deals weren't really settled until my father took over."

"So, they're big accounts?"

He nodded while he scrolled. "I just don't know why each of them are so far behind."

I scratched my head, staring at the desk. There was an envelope sitting open. Vito's seal was broken on it, and there looked like there was light writing on the inside flap.

Vito's phone rang out, drawing my attention away from the envelope.

"Hello?" He placed the phone on speaker so we could all hear.

"Boss? It's bad. Leo was out sick, and no one was on cameras, and it's not looking good." Logan sounded concerned and distraught. The nerves returned, and I was sinking into a pit of anxiety. Someone had infiltrated BT and had taken Iyana. She could be dead, and it was all my fault.

"I should've been here," I whispered to the floor.

"We don't have time for that." Vito slapped my shoulder on his way out.

"I should've been here," I whispered again. I lifted my gaze to the desk, and that envelope caught my eye again. Before taking my leave, I grabbed it and headed down to meet Logan and Vito.

We met inside the camera room. Kat was sitting at a desk, replaying something to Vito and Logan who were huddled around her. I stepped closer and watched the screen. Iyana burst from Vito's apartment, racing down the hall. She looked like she was screaming, but before she could make it to the elevators, she was tackled. The dark figure stood to his feet and began dragging her back towards Vito's apartment. I turned away when I recognized the figure.

It was Brandon.

"Do we have any outdoor footage?" Vito asked calmly.

"We only had this," Kat said. But I wouldn't look, I didn't want to see Iyana's lifeless body being dragged around.

"But we were able to tap into the street camera," she went on.

Slowly, I turned to see what the street camera picked up. Brandon's car zipped out the Tower's lot and headed east.

"East," I whispered. Everyone turned and looked at me, and I waved my hands. "One time, Brandon had me go as far east until we reached a warehouse."

"A warehouse?" Vito came over to me. "When? Where?"

"A while back when I was still his driver. I can't remember, but I know the only directions were to go east."

Vito nodded and took a breath. "I'm only going to ask once," he said calmly. Before I knew it, the air was gushed from stomach, and I dropped to one knee. Raising my head, it was met with the coolness of Vito's gun barrel.

"Are you a traitor?"

I shook my head. "No, Vito, I swear. I've never betrayed you. I don't know about anything that's going on."

He pressed the gun harder into my head, and I squeezed my eyes closed. For only the second time in my entire life, I pleaded with God. The first was when I was taken from school, I asked Him to spare me. This would be the second time I begged for His mercy.

"If you're lying to me," Vito seethed into my ear, "I will not let you die. I will do everything I can to keep you alive, to live through the torture I'm going to do to you." He ripped the gun from my head and said hotly, "Get up. You're driving me to this warehouse."

Shakily I stood to my feet, whispering gratitude to God.

"What's that in your hand?" Kat said as she moved from her desk.

"It's an envelope I got from Iyana's desk. It's empty, it just has something written on it." I passed it to Vito, and he gasped.

His brows lowered as he said, "Why did she have this? Where did she get this from?"

"I don't know," I answered. "The name on the side, it was written on a sticky note on Iyana's desk. She unscrambled the word, and it was 'Morenos.'"

"So what?" Logan said, crossing his arms.

"So, I think it has something to do with whatever was inside of it. And…" I stopped, staring at the envelope in his hand.

"And what?" Vito asked.

"And I've delivered some of those envelopes for Brandon. I didn't know what they were; he would just put them in the pile of mail, and I'd deliver them. I swear I didn't—"

"I know," Vito said, looking at the envelope, "he must've done the same to Iyana. Asked her to seal these to trick people."

"Trick people? What do you mean?"

Logan and Vito exchanged a look before Vito explained, "This isn't the first envelope like this or the first report since the rat. I started doing some visits to clients because Iyana said they were missing payments." He took a deep breath, keeping his face void of all emotion; he only blinked at the envelope.

"None of them had this writing on the inside. At least, I don't think so."

"That would make sense," I said.

Kat crossed her arms. "Why?"

"Because, the rat, or Brandon," I said gently, "is giving information, money and resources to Grizzly, right? He probably couldn't convince every legendary account to move, so he started thieving from smaller people to bring Grizzly something."

"But what's his motive?" Logan shrugged.

"I don't know," I said slowly, "but that warehouse, this name on the envelope, and those letters are all connected."

"The letter gave the clients an address to send their payments, they all went to that warehouse," Vito said.

"I see now." Kat stepped forward. "He's after the big accounts, right?"

I nodded.

"That would crush BT, wouldn't it?"

"Yeah," Vito said.

"There's the motive. Grizzly has given him an impossible task, take down BT," Kat announced.

"But why?" I asked. "Why take us down for Grizzly?"

"I don't know," Kat admitted, "but this is a start."

"I still don't understand the name on the inside flap," Logan spoke up. "Why would he scramble a name on the inside of an envelope?"

Vito rubbed his chin. "Because that's the next location for the Stoll's payment. Instead of sending them to the warehouse, he's sending them to the Morenos, and that's where he'll get their payments."

The only sound in the room was that of our pounding hearts and stirring minds. Brandon had played us all, but especially Vito. Vito had given Brandon all his trust, and Brandon cashed in on that trust, and nearly took BT down.

"We've got to get moving," Vito said after the silence had mounted to near suffocation. "Logan, take your own vehicle and come through the front, Hardy and I will go through the back. Kat—"

"Yes?" she answered promptly.

"Get the video footage of what happened between last shift and this shift. Get some people you trust up to Iyana's place to clean up the bodies, and I want you searching our empty apartments for bodies, including mine."

"Understood." She nodded.

"So, does this mean a war has started?" I asked.

"No," Vito said. "As long as I get Iyana back, I won't make mention of the men I lost. I'll replace them and let it go. There's no need for a war."

"Understood," we all said.

"And, Kat, lock down the Tower," he said darkly. "I don't want anyone in or out."

7

The Lone Bullet

I inhaled deeply and rolled over. My hands were behind my back.

Shaking the grogginess from my head, I tugged on my hands. The rattling of chains rang out and I sat up quickly and looked around. I was in a warehouse of some sort. All kinds of drugs were sitting around; weed, cocaine, pills, and even piles of money were stacked high.

"Where am I?" I whispered.

"You're awake," the cunning voice of Brandon rippled through the warehouse.

"Why?" I shouted as he came into view. He was wearing a smirk like everything was a joke. "Why did you do this to us?"

"Whoa?" He squinted. "*Us?* Since when were you part of BT, Iyana? Last time I checked, you were trying to find your way out."

"I'm still part of it until I'm gone."

"So, you *are* still trying to get away? Because I can offer you a spot at Grizzly's. A mind like yours is really needed there." He paused and rubbed his chin. "They lack knowledge, I guess. And any means of getting it. They're archaic, in a way. I don't know how to describe it."

"I don't understand why you'd do something like this." I tried not to let my voice shake, but the mounting heartbreak was almost unbearable. "Vito trusted you. *I* trusted you."

"You *never* trusted me, Iyana! It was just a matter of time until you figured out that I was the rat. Picking you up ruined my plans." He shook his head. "I was so close to handing BT over to Grizzly on a silver platter before you showed up. But Vito just wouldn't kill you."

"Because he actually has a heart!" I shouted.

Brandon fell back in laughter, cradling his abdomen. "Vito," he snorted, "a *heart*? Please! The man has killed more people than his father. Some he just killed because he could. Others to prove a point, but there were hardly any he killed for safety reasons or self-defense. Vito is a cold-blooded murderer. Just like everyone in this business."

"That's not true," I whimpered as tears came to my eyes. "You're wrong about Vito. He's not like that at all."

"Aww..." He placed big hands over his heart. "Do you feel something for him? Does Iyana have a little crush on the leader of the notorious Woof Pack? How charming."

"What's wrong with you, Brandon? How could you betray

your own brother?"

"Brother? If Vito thought of me as a real brother, I would be running the entire gang by now. He let me manage five measly accounts, and only because the clients didn't want to work with him."

"So, you turned on him for power?"

"I turned on him because I know he's going to turn on me."

I pulled into myself. "What do you mean?"

He shrugged and pulled his gun out. "I guess I'll tell you before you die. I can't have someone like you running around and telling Vito all my plans."

"I'm not stupid. I know you took me to lure Vito here so you can kill him."

He smiled, what was once so charming had somehow become dark and menacing.

"I do want to kill Vito, but not quite yet. I still need to acquire some accounts from him to convince Grizzly of my loyalty."

"I just don't know why you would betray him. He loved you."

"Not this again," he grumbled. "I told you; it was a matter of time before he turned on me."

"A matter of time? He hadn't turned on you in all this time, why would he now?" I tried to remain still as I twisted my wrists against the cuffs, trying to squeeze one of my hands out.

Brandon looked distant for a moment, looking off at the cannabis, he said quietly, "He never even yelled at me for it."

I squinted. "For what?"

"For getting Jewels pregnant. He never got angry, didn't make me quit, he never even got rid of Jewels. It was like none of it mattered to him."

I chuckled, shaking my head. "You're scared that Vito's waiting for a moment to kill you."

"I'm not scared of anything. And you'd better watch your mouth," he said darkly. But I needed this, I needed him talking. Even if he hit me, that would buy me more time, and hopefully Vito would notice me gone soon and come looking for me.

I took a deep breath and lifted my head. *God, please get me out of this...*

"It's funny, evil people are always the ones with the most to live for. The ones who don't want to die. They always want a second chance."

"You don't know what you're talking about," he snapped.

"I think I do," I said firmly. "You knew what you did was wrong, but you can't figure out why you didn't get the punishment you so deserved."

"I don't want to hear this," he said as he turned to leave.

"But you should!" I called. "It figures you wouldn't want to hear the truth, though. You don't want to hear how much of a coward you are by sneaking around behind Vito's back and sleeping with his girl. He gave you a second chance to make things right and look at what you've done."

"If you say anything else, I'm going to shoot you!"

I laughed nervously, wondering how much longer I could keep this up. I forced myself to hold back the anxious tears that were burning my eyes and said, "You're absolutely nothing, Brandon. And I trusted you."

He thundered across the room to me, and I backed up until I hit the wall. He snatched me up by my hair and I cried out.

"I said *be quiet*." He threw me back to the floor, my chains clattering against it as I fell back down. I raised my eyes to look at his tall figure.

"I don't have to take this from you or anyone else," he snapped. "We are making a fortune off Vito's products and we're changing Jersey. It's just a matter of time until we reach New York."

"We?" I snorted and reeled back. "*We?*" I exclaimed louder.

His eyes darkened and his lips sagged until he frowned.

"We?" I said again with a smirk. "Grizzly doesn't even trust you. There is no *we*."

He leaned down and I could feel his breath on my cheeks as he sneered, "I am going to earn his trust."

"Just to betray him and get to the top?"

With the back of his gun, he whipped my face. I fell over to floor as the pain burst in my cheek. Slowly, I dragged myself back upright as he panted over me.

"You know…" I swallowed. "This is all a game for Grizzly. He's got you working like a mule. Stealing and thieving for Gang Grizzly, but you don't even belong there. Why do you think he turned you in? Now you don't belong to Grizzly *or* Vito! You've got no protection, Brandon! You're all alone. You're powerless."

"Shut up!" he cried as he pistol-whipped me again. "You have no idea what you're talking about! Everything I've done has been for me! Not Grizzly, so I don't care if he never trusts me."

"That's a lie!" I shouted.

Brandon punched me to the floor, and I gasped as I laid there, waiting for him to step away. Slowly, I turned over and spat blood onto the concrete floor. I wanted to give up, to die right then, but I knew I could hold on a little longer. Brandon was clearly waiting on Vito, but I didn't know how long he'd wait. But I wanted Vito to catch him to clear his name to the clients who wanted to back out of BT because they thought there was an uncontrollable rat problem, but I needed him talking to keep him here.

"Do these accounts know you're working for Grizzly?" My words were slurred, but from his dark laughter, I figured he understood.

"Some of them know, two of them don't. But once I get—"

"I lied," I said quietly. "I lied about the Abletons."

For a single second, I'm certain Brandon's heart stopped. In the next second he was dragging me from the floor up to his face by my shirt.

"What did you say?"

"I said, I lied about the Abletons. I know things about them that I've never told you or Vito. But now, I think I'll tell him."

His hand went to my throat, and he squeezed it tightly.

"Tell me now, or so help me God, I will kill you!"

Hawking up as much blood as I could, I spat it into his face. He blinked twice, and then lost control. I was shoved to the ground with both his hands wrapped around my throat. I kicked and thrashed, trying to get him off of me. My hands were still behind my back, but I fought anyway. I was determined not to die. Tears spilled from my eyes as rage ignited in Brandon's. That uneasy feeling I always got around him was now overwhelming as I thrashed against him.

Mercifully, God sent help.

Two gunshots went off, and Brandon released me. I rolled over, coughing violently onto the floor as he raised his gun.

"Vito!" I hollered. "Logan! Anyone! I'm here!"

Two more gunshots went off, and Brandon took off in their direction. I sat up quickly, trying to see what was happening when someone came up behind me and covered my mouth. I tried to scream but the person whispered, "I'm sorry I wasn't there, Iyana. I'm a lousy guard, but I still found you."

He lowered his hand and I cried, "Hardy!"

He was jiggling the cuffs when more gunfire went off. "Hardy what's going on?"

"Logan's having a shootout with Brandon."

"Is Vito here?"

"Yeah," he whispered, "he's setting a perimeter."

"A perimeter?"

"Of gasoline. He's going to blow this place up." He paused and looked at his watch. "We've got a minute and thirty-three seconds if we're not out…"

A cuff popped open, and I turned over to hug Hardy. "Thank you for coming for me."

"We don't have time." He pushed me back and snatched my other wrist. Popping the other cuff off, he grabbed my hand and we raced to an exit when someone else fired at us.

"Get down!" Hardy screamed as he dragged me to the floor. Another shot went off as he held me against his chest. "On my count!"

Two more shots fired off behind us, making me jump.

"I'm going to rush the guy ahead of us, you come right behind me and head for the exit."

I nodded. "Be careful."

He grabbed my arm as gunfire continued to go off. "One ... Two ... Three!"

We sprang to our feet, and Hardy fired as he ran forward. I stayed on his heels, running toward the man who was shooting at us. He was reloading when Hardy tackled him to the ground.

"Go!" he shouted to me.

I jumped over the two of them tussling and sprinted to the exit. I rushed outside, but there was no one out front. Racing around the other side of the building, I saw Vito holding a book of matches.

"Vito!" I screamed as I ran. "Someone else showed up! He's fighting with Hardy!"

Vito met me halfway and grabbed my arm. "Come on! You have to get in the car."

We raced for it just as Logan darted out of the side

entrance. There were two guys on his tail, but Vito fired at them, and they ran sideways, trying to dodge the shots. Logan took the opportunity and raced for his car.

"Get inside! Go!" he screamed as he ripped open his car door.

Two men backed off and turned back for the building. As I climbed inside the truck, I screamed, "Where's Hardy!? He's still in there!"

"I know, we have to—"

Two shots went off and then there was silence.

I gripped Vito's arm as I stared out the window at the warehouse. Slowly, the side door opened, and Hardy came limping out with a gun in his hand. His eyes were wide, and he was panting. But not because he was tired, he was in shock. Hardy had killed someone; he'd killed a member of Gang Grizzly…

He'd started a war.

8

Where Do You Belong

"He killed one of our men, Grizzly."

The old man harrumphed in his seat as he pulled a cigar from his lips. "*Our* men?"

I swallowed. "*Your* men, Grizzly."

"That's right." He nodded. "One of my men was killed because of you, and now," he placed his cigar between his lips again, "now I'm part of a gang war."

"I … I'm sorry. I can make this right."

There was a stillness in the room, one that was frightening. I hated working for Grizzly. He was as reckless as Mr. Gerardo, Vito's father. When a smaller gang launched an attack on BT under Mr. Gerardo, his wife was the one that ended up getting attacked instead, and it made him paranoid and unfit to be the head of BT. He wanted to step down, but he had no heir so he couldn't.

I was the perfect fit for BT. I was going to make the gang better than it had ever been. But Mr. Gerardo didn't think so. Even when I came to him and showed him my plans, he never even considered me. He thought I'd support the gang better as *second* in charge. But I didn't want to be second, I wanted to be first.

"How exactly can you make this right, Brandon?" Grizzly shouted as he stood abruptly. His loud voice pulled me from the dark thoughts clouding my mind. I often escaped there when I had to deal with Grizzly. He treated me like trash, and I hated it. But until I could take his seat, I'd have to suffer a bit longer.

I sighed and rubbed a hand over my head. "We've got plenty of money and—"

"Manpower! You idiot! We don't have manpower!" He leaned forward, the fur around his collar shifting with his movement. "Money cannot buy manpower—not *loyal* manpower."

"But, Grizzly, they killed one of us."

"Stop saying *us*!" He took his cigar and tossed it across the room. "Until my gang wins this war, there is no *us*, Brandon! There's you and there's Gang Grizzly and BT! That's it."

I almost let myself remember Iyana's words, how she'd said almost the exact same thing to me, but instead, I cleared my throat and said, "BT killed one of your members. Which means you have time to retaliate, and they can't do anything about it. You get one week to retaliate; something could be done in that time."

He wrinkled his nose as he sat down in his chair. "A week to retaliate when we have nothing."

"We do—" I cut myself off when I noticed his dark gaze scowling at me. "*You* still have options. You may not have manpower, but you do have intelligence. You can 'legally' take one of his businesses during this time, and he can't do anything about it."

"Until their week to retaliate," he said, sitting back in his chair, contemplating the unspoken laws of gang life. We might be thugs, but there is a system—a code—that we live by. Killing members from another gang gives the other group the option to respond accordingly; they typically have a week to make a move.

"Maybe I won't retaliate. He was just a cub anyway. New to the gang, he didn't matter."

A feeling of raw hatred stirred in my chest for Vito. He didn't work hard for anything he got, and yet he has a whole different gang across state lines cowering to him.

Woof Pack has always been intimidating because of the way they do business. They're friendly, they're trustworthy, they don't hurt people for no reason, despite the lies I told Iyana about Vito. He doesn't outwardly rule with fear, which is something people have always liked about him—mostly because they don't know him. They don't realize every man is two-sided, and blindly they love him. But I have always hated that love he gloats in because he knows the truth.

Ruling the underworld with fake kindness is stupid. We're

in a gang, there's illegal activity going on all day every day, handling things with sympathy seemed like an atrocity to me. That's why I started working with Grizzly. It was time for a new era of gangs to rise. A new era of brute strength, not the hidden kind only used when needed.

Peace was getting old; everyone had an itch to shoot something. I wanted to scratch that itch, but I couldn't if Grizzly was just going to cower to Vito. He played nice and he played by the rules, just like the binding of a book. But in reality, on the inside of that book, Vito had broken every rule, or had enough power to bend the rules or make his own. He had a way of setting fear into the hearts of rival gangs because you really can't judge a book by its cover.

"Grizzly," I said firmly as I took a step toward his desk. He shot me a glare that froze me in my step. You weren't allowed to approach the cove of Grizzly without his permission. It was enough I was allowed in, but to get in closer could mean disrespect.

"You can't let this go or they'll keep trying to take things from you."

"Like the way you've taken things from them?"

I stiffened. When I first started working for Grizzly, it was right after I tried to start my own gang in the crevices of New York. My partner was found out and skinned by Gerardo himself. So, I laid low for a while until I bumped into Grizzly. He'd crossed over into NYC turf, Vito's turf, and I should've turned him in. But I saw an opportunity to take over his small gang and make it better, so I offered him some of Vito's resources. I figured I'd need them once I took his place and, really, I began setting up Gang Grizzly to my liking.

Grizzly asked me one day why I was betraying Vito, the Gerardos, and Woof Pack. I told him my full potential to lead the pack was being disregarded, and he asked if I was trying to lead his den. I lied and told him I was tired of the way Vito ran things, the second chances he gave, he didn't show real power, but Grizzly did.

I mused over the conversation in my head as I stood before Grizzly's dimly lit room. Brown wooden floors, animal skins all over, with a grand picture of a grizzly bear tearing apart its prey.

"Grizzly," I said in the quiet, "everything I've done has been what you've asked me to do. I've killed, I've stolen, I've brought you clients, money, and products. When are you going to start trusting me?"

"Trust you? You want me to trust you after everything you've done to Vito? Your *brother*?"

A knot formed in my stomach, and I squeezed my hands closed.

"You betrayed your own kin for power, for anger, for fear, or whatever unclear reason in your head. And you expect me to trust you?"

"Everything," I whispered through a clenched jaw, "*everything* I did was for you and this gang. Do you really think I would've given up my cushy life for this? For running around with no safety, no security from you?"

He sighed and stretched out his legs as he leaned back in

his chair. "Just get me a business during this week, and we'll go from there for the future of this war." He paused and raised his old, tired face. "When did gangs get so political? A bloodless war is upon us… I can feel it."

I nodded and left Grizzly's cove.

I got in my truck and drove off down the highway. Grizzly was giving me another chance to make things right after my incredible screw up at the warehouse. I expected Vito to come with Logan, but I didn't expect Hardy. I didn't think he trusted him yet, but it seems like Vito is as gullible as his father, as trusting as him. That worked for me, since Grizzly still didn't know how much Iyana meant to Vito. I could use that as leverage for myself.

If I can capture Iyana again and leave her somewhere close to Grizzly's territory, he may come after Grizzly, and I won't have to get my hands dirty.

I pulled into my driveway and hopped out the car. The front door opened, and Brandon junior waved frantically from the porch. I smiled, as I approached the steps, carrying a gift box for him.

"Daddy!" he exclaimed as I opened the screen door.

"BJ!" I leaned down and scooped him up in one arm. He wrapped his arms around me and hugged me tight.

"Is that for me?" he asked as I put him down.

"It is." I lowered the wrapped present to him. "But it goes under the tree."

"Aww, Dad, come on!"

"Sorry, BJ, you know how your mother feels about gifts.

They're all a secret."

He blew air between his lips before scurrying off.

I found Alex, my wife, in the kitchen making dinner. "Good evening," I said, wrapping my arms around her waist.

She purred, "Good evening, Brandon. You're late again."

I tapped her bottom before walking to the fridge and opening it. "I know. This job transfer to this new location is kicking my butt." I pulled out a bottle of cranberry juice and looked it over.

"You want to talk about it?" Alex asked as she turned to face me.

"Nah. It's just work. You know, same old checks and balances, accounts and all that boring stuff. Just making sure the accounts I worked on at the old firm are set; all their info and data is transferring over to my new firm."

She smiled, twisting the silver spatula in her sugar brown hand. "Alright, whatever you say."

"Come on, Lex," I said after drinking some cranberry juice. "I don't want you stressing with our baby on the way."

She rolled her eyes and started flipping over the patties in the skillet.

"You're not seriously upset, right?"

She shook her head, dark curls shaking with the movement.

"Yes, you are. Why are you upset?" I closed the fridge and moved around the kitchen, throwing my tie on the granite counter, and unbuttoning my shirt.

"You never want to tell me anything about your job, Bee.

I don't like that."

Alex has always pestered me about work. She means well, trying to be part of my life, but she just doesn't need to know about my real job. About how we can afford a million-dollar home, and really anything we wanted. She thinks I work at a firm on Wall Street, that I trade stocks, and run numbers. I sighed as I sat on a barstool, watching her make dinner.

"I work in an industry where everything is a secret, Alex. I don't know what to tell you. Client information cannot be shared."

"So, there's nothing at all you can share with me?"

"No." I shrugged.

She slammed the spatula down and snapped, "I know you're lying, Bee!"

I glared at her as I stood slowly.

She immediately cleared her throat and waved a hand. "I'm sorry. I'm just hormonal and stressed." Tears were forming in her eyes, and I sighed away my annoyance with her outburst.

"Alex, what's really going on?"

She took a deep breath and whispered, "Today, BJ asked me if his little sister will look more like me because she's a girl. I've just been really emotional about it all day."

If there was one person in the world I loved, it was Alex. She was my anchor, she was everything to me, and I'd do anything to protect her. Keeping my gang affiliation a secret was good for her, the less she knew, the better, or at least it was easier for me that way.

"What did you say to him?"

"I just told him 'yes.' I didn't want to try to point out things that were similar between us, because there isn't anything there." She shook her head. "He's six now, in a few years he's going to start noticing our differences, especially with a little sister."

"I know, but it's fine. We'll deal with it."

"When, Brandon? Because he's going to wonder where his real mom is at some point, and what am I supposed to say?"

"The truth," I stressed. "Tell him the truth. His mother died in childbirth, and you've been in his life since he was almost two. That's it."

She pushed away from me and grabbed her skillet. "The food's burned." She sighed, twisting off the stove eye. "You make it sound so easy. But I'm not the one who should have to tell him this."

I tsked her and crossed back to the barstool. It was true, but I'd never admit it.

"We'll deal with it, alright? Let's just order pizza tonight," I said as I pulled out my phone.

She rolled her eyes and left the kitchen.

9

Facades and Truths

"Morning, Lex and BJ, I'm going out of town again for the weekend, so you guys don't need to wait up for me."

"Wait a second," Alex said, "BJ's little league championship is on Saturday. You've already missed almost half the season, you cannot miss this," she stressed.

BJ nervously adjusted in his chair as he continued to scribble in his coloring book. "It's alright, Mommy," he said, sinking his head to his hand. "Daddy's busy."

I blinked, wondering just how many more times I'd blink and he'd be another year older, another achievement he's attained, more success that I've missed.

"You know what," I crossed over to BJ, "I'll probably have some time off on Saturday. I might be able to make it to your game."

"Really?" His eyes glowed with cheer, and my chest tightened so abruptly, I almost coughed. I never knew how much he cared or loved me. I didn't know he ever paid my presence any attention. It was gut-wrenching to see my own son happy at the *chance* that his father would be at his championship game.

"Yeah." I swallowed the tears that pricked my eyes. "I'm going to do my best to be there. So, make sure you look for me in the crowd, alright?" He nodded as he jumped from his seat and came around to hug me. I glanced over at Alex, and she mouthed, 'thank you.'

"Alright, BJ, I've got to go now. So, I'll see you at the game."

"Okay!" he shouted with a wave.

Alex walked me to the front door where we exchanged a kiss more passionate than the last few times we'd kissed.

"He's really counting on this, Bee, don't let him down."

I nodded. Her hazel eyes always melted me. I think I fell in love with the way she looked at me before I even knew her name.

"I'm going to do my best."

"He doesn't understand that, especially if you don't make it." She poked my chest with each word. "So. Make. It."

I took a long pause, studying my wife. "Alright, I'll be there."

She kissed me once more before I left.

On my way to the warehouse, I sent a text to Jewels to meet me there. It was nine in the morning, and I knew she was probably still sleep, but she was the only one who could buy me the time I'd need on Saturday to get to Junior's game. Her text came back slow, but she said she'd meet me there in an hour. I also needed to discuss future plans with her so we could get more intel on BT. With me gone now, I needed her, and whatever other guards who hadn't been found out, to get information on accounts and BT as a whole.

As I pulled up, Brooke and Dahodda stood out front smoking. I'd set them on guard since Vito and BT now knew where I was keeping some of the products stashed; I didn't know when they'd be back to try to blow the place up or steal from it.

"What are you two doing?" I said as I walked up to them.

Dahodda and Brooke were brothers from the Bronx. Brooke was nineteen, Dahodda was eighteen, and they'd been in the streets selling drugs since Brooke was sixteen. I pulled them off the street for myself before Vito found them. Young bucks were the best for the industry. They were ignorant with nothing but dollar signs in their eyes. Their loyalty was fiercer because they feared the police, and they enjoyed the money they earned. I learned that from Vito when he recruited Logan, and then Hardy. Both were young, but both needed help.

Hardy was a smart kid we took for ransom, but when his mother killed herself, Vito kept him. Gave him a job, and a place to stay, he basically bought his loyalty. He'd already worked the formula on Logan when he recruited him off the streets. Things were a little different with Logan, though. He and Vito actually developed a brotherhood, they became close, closer than Vito and I had become. But even so, Vito still respected me because of his father, and he never put Logan over me. Logan worked for Vito and me equally, even though I knew Vito wanted Logan to be his personal assistant, he never kept him from me.

"We're guarding," Dahodda said as he blew a smoke ring at me. I fanned it and snatched the blunt from his hand, and then snatched his brother's smoke.

"How many times do I have to tell you two not to smoke the product?"

I threw down the blunts and stamped them out into the snow.

"Come on," Brooke whined.

"No!" I snapped. "I keep telling you two that you can't smoke what we sell."

"No one's going to notice! It's just *two* blunts." Dahodda shrugged.

"It doesn't matter. That all adds up if you're doing it all the time!"

He raised his hands defensively. "Alright, we got it. Chill."

I squinted and stepped toward him. "*Chill?* Boy do you know how much trouble I could be in? Do you know how much money I'm losing every time you two decide you're bored and want to smoke something that doesn't belong to you? That weed is already paid for by clients! What am I supposed to tell them?"

"We're sorry!" Brooke shouted. "Please, he's just a hothead. But I promise we won't do it again. This is better than the streets. Hodda, we can't mess this up."

Dahodda grunted and shoved his hands into his pockets.

"Good," I said, passing a look between them both. "I'm going inside, let Jewels in when she shows up."

"Understood," Brooke said.

I knew Jewels would take more than an hour, so I started making arrangements for the trimmers to come in before Christmas and be done by New Years. Grizzly was getting their first shipment from a cannabis farm I'd heard of from working for Vito. They were cheaper, but the weedheads in Jersey wouldn't know the difference. They liked the illegal activity more than they enjoyed the leaf itself.

"You rang," the thumping of Jewels's boots brought her over to my desk in the back of the warehouse.

"Glad you could make it," I said, leaning over the desk to kiss her.

She walked around the desk to look me in the eye. "Before you start asking favors, have you heard anything from your mom?"

I raised a brow. "From my mom? No, why?"

She slumped her shoulders, her purse sagging forward. "I thought she may have been able to do it, that's all." She shook her head. "I don't like him staying in an adoption center. It's not right."

I closed my eyes for a second when I realized she was talking about BJ.

"Oh! No, my mother has actually set up an appointment, she's going to adopt him."

Her mouth dropped open and she didn't say anything for a few moments.

"You're serious," she whispered, swiping at a falling tear. "He's going to have a home? After six long years…"

"I told you I'd take care of him. You just have to trust me, Jewels."

She nodded as I leaned forward and kissed her again. "Thank you, Brandon. I'm so glad our son will have a real home now."

I forced the widest smile I could because I needed her to do me a big favor, so I had to fake this one well. "Me too. Six years is too long for a child to be homeless."

She nodded as she dabbed her eyes. "It is. But he won't be soon enough."

She set her purse on my desk and slowly unbuttoned her jacket. It fell to the floor in a heap, but I didn't pay it any attention, I was too distracted by the sheer shirt she had on—with no bra underneath. Her shorts were so tight, her thighs spilled from beneath them. Jewels was the sexiest woman I knew. Even sexier than Alex. I loved Alex, more than anything and anyone, but she wasn't part of this lifestyle, she wasn't part of this world. She didn't know the things Jewels knew about me, and that made me feel connected to Jewels.

She stepped out of her boots and pushed me back into my chair. In one swift motion, she straddled me, wrapped her arms around my neck, and kissed me hard. The appreciation and desperation spilled from her lips with every kiss, and I loved the taste of it, but today was day two, and I only had five more to bring one of Vito's clients to my side. That shouldn't be a problem as long as I could make a good enough argument, but I still needed to prepare for it.

"Jewels," I said, pulling away.

"What?" she whispered playfully.

"We can't do this right now."

"Why not? Dahodda and Brooke have heard us before. Who cares?" She went back to kissing my neck.

"Jewels, I'm in a bind, and I've got to do something soon."

She froze, slowly pulling her lips from my neck. "Right, you only ever call me here for a favor," she said flatly.

"You're the only one I can ask."

She rolled her eyes and climbed off me.

"Jewels, they killed a member of Gang Grizzly. We have to retaliate."

"Why? I don't even understand what you've been doing, Brandon. BT was your home. It's my home. And if I get put out, I'll have nowhere to go."

"You won't get put out; you'll be fine."

She placed a hand on her hip. "What do you need me to do?"

"Befriend Iyana and get information out of her about accounts. And I need you to keep Grizzly busy this Saturday."

"What? Why?"

I chewed my lip, trying to think of a lie. I'd forgotten to put one together before she showed up. I couldn't tell her I was going to BJ's game, but I needed it to be believable.

"I'm going with my mom to the adoption center to help

fill out the forms and get everything set up. It's a long process, and I need to be there to help her out."

She softened just a little, but she still snapped when she asked, "What am I supposed to do?"

"I don't know, Jewels, whatever you want. Just keep him busy for a few hours. You know Grizzly likes you."

She shook her head and grabbed her things to leave.

"Where are you going?" I snapped.

"Incredible how you always find time for me when you need me." She tossed her jacket over her shoulders and snatched her purse.

"So, what, you're not going to do it? After everything?"

She stopped and looked over her shoulder, her broken heart was spilling from her eyes. "When have I ever *not* come through?" She turned on her heels and left me there to stare in silence.

10

Home

"How is she?" I asked as I stepped into the penthouse. I hadn't been home since the shootout yesterday. I sent Hardy home to care for Iyana while Logan and I visited some clients and made last minute travel arrangements. With a war at hand, unlike any war before, I'd need all the help I could get.

"She's awake—if that's what you're asking, boss," Hardy replied.

I nodded as I passed him to head to the bedroom, but he called out to me, "Boss?"

"Why the formality all of a sudden? You hardly ever call me 'boss,'" I said with my back to him. I stared ahead at the paintings on my wall as Hardy tried to find the words to say.

"I'm sorry. I didn't mean to shoot him. We were tussling and things go out of control and the gun went off."

Was I angry? I was infuriated, but there was nothing to be done now. The war had begun, and I had a week to prepare for all the possibilities.

"Just keep an eye out for Logan."

I left him and headed into the bedroom. Iyana was sitting up in bed, a busted lip, and a gash across her cheek. She was in horrible shape. She shifted uncomfortably under my gaze, trying to pull the blankets over her scraped wrists.

"How are you?" I asked as I crossed the room to her.

"I could ask you the same. Have you slept at all?"

I chuckled and sat on the edge of her bed. "I'm fine."

"Vito," her voice was gentle and kind like it'd always been, "your brother was the rat."

Her words were like daggers in my already throbbing chest. I was trying not to think about Brandon as the rat, as the one who'd been selling me out to Gang Grizzly, but it was an inevitable conversation, inevitable thoughts that would be lingering for ages to come.

We sat in silence, and I remembered this feeling all too well, except last time I felt this way, I didn't have anyone by my side. I was alone to figure out my feelings, figure out how in the world I would move beyond my own brother sleeping with the woman I was with. But, little by little, it got easier until one day, I'd forgotten that had even happened despite how much it changed our relationship.

"Brandon stopped trusting me a while ago," I said softly. "He didn't know why I forgave him, or why I didn't take my anger out on him. And in his confusion, he stopped trusting me. He started to believe I would someday use what he did against him."

"It's funny," she said, "how showing kindness and forgiving someone could have the total opposite effect than you intended. It's like people somehow *want* to be punished, and when they aren't, they never accept their forgiveness. They never believe you've truly left their sins behind."

"Yeah, something like that."

There was silence again, just the sound of my racing heart pounding in my ears. I shook my head as I stood to my feet. "I can't think about this right now. I need you to get a bag packed and be ready in the next twenty minutes." I headed for the door.

"What? Why?"

"Because a war just started, and I've got to focus on that. We're going to need help to keep this war bloodless."

--- BT ---

We stepped off the jet and was greeted by the sweltering sun of California. I'd told Iyana to dress for the summer, but on the ride over, she stayed in her winter garments, so I was forced to wait in the airport for her to change with Challa. She'd brought him along since they'd never been separated before, and she said it would be good for Challa to go see other places. I didn't care one way or another, and the place we were going wouldn't, either.

"Ok," Iyana's voice came over my shoulder, "sorry, that

took longer than expected."

I whirled around and froze. It felt like the winter chill of New York had somehow made it here to Los Angeles. Iyana has always been gorgeous but in the skintight clothes Jewels gave her, she looked like something from my wildest dream.

Her round hips and full breasts were stuffed into a tiny little baby pink dress. It stopped at the thigh, allowing me to bear witness to her smooth legs. Her lips were a nude color, and she wore simple makeup that covered her bruises with waist-length braids.

I am a man of God...

"Vito?" she called with a raised brow, and suddenly the heat of LA was washing over me.

"Yeah, let's go," I muttered as I pulled on Challa's leash.

"Are you alright?" she asked as we made our way through the airport. "You were staring at me like you'd spaced out."

"Oh..." I chuckled nervously. "Well ... I just ..." I paused but she filled in words for me that I didn't deny or agree with.

"I know Brandon's the rat, but you said we were here to get help, right? So, just try not to think about it."

I nodded as we made it outdoors. There was a driver already waiting for us, holding a sign that read: **Ortega**.

"Ortega? Isn't that the name you used on your fake ID?" Iyana asked once we got into a black car.

"Yeah, you remember?" I asked, watching Challa get comfortable in his own seat.

She nodded. "So that means I'll be misses Ortega while I'm here?" Her cheeks flushed red as she blinked up at me.

I couldn't help myself. The heat, and her short dress, her blinking eyes, everything was taking a toll on my fragile heart and, without thinking, I leaned down and grazed her neck with my lips. I didn't want to kiss it because if I did, I might go too far.

"Do you want to be?" I whispered.

She giggled but didn't answer. My hand slipped to her leg, but then I stopped, reminding myself that I wasn't a hormonal teenager in the back of the car on prom night. I was here to do business because there was a war at home, and I needed to protect Iyana and BT. But I also remembered that she isn't the *real* Mrs. Ortega. That meant I couldn't do what I wanted to do.

I sat back against the seat and sighed, cracking my window as the driver came around the front. "It is nice to see you again, Mr. Ortega," he said as he adjusted his mirror.

"It's been a while, Henry, thanks for having me."

He nodded. "It's always a pleasure, sir. Where to?"

"Home," I said.

He smiled. "Are they expecting you, sir?"

"It'll be a surprise for everyone."

He nodded again. "What a wonderful surprise, sir. Home it is."

I turned to Iyana who'd been watching the exchange. She raised a brow and looked up at me, "What do you mean *home?*"

I hadn't told her everything, just enough to get us out of the tower as quickly as possible. And she'd slept on the jet, so I didn't get the chance to tell her anything, but now was as good a time as any before she met my family.

"You know Mr. Gerardo ... he was the leader of BT before me."

She nodded.

"So I need his help with this new problem." I glanced at Henry and back at Iyana.

She picked up on my discretion and said, "So we're here to ask your father for help?"

"Yes."

Her forehead wrinkled, and she leaned her head back against the seats in total dismay.

"What's wrong?" I stared at her face, but I couldn't keep my eyes on hers, they shot down her neck to rove over the rest of her body before sliding back up to her face before she caught me.

"I'm going to meet your family in the dirty clothes you make me wear."

Henry cleared his throat loudly, but I refused to look up at him.

"Ana," I said roughly, "there are things that you can say, and things you can't say while you're here."

"You don't want me telling your family about the slut fantasy you have?" she barked.

I grunted. "Iyana, please stop."

She shook her head. "You should've told me where we were going!"

"*Lower* your voice," I snapped.

She rolled her eyes, and I grabbed her wrist, pulling her

closer to me. "You cannot behave like this in front of my family. Got it?"

She snatched her wrist from me and snarled, "All you had to do was tell me where we were going, and I wouldn't have dressed like the dirty office slut you want me to be."

"Can you please stop saying that word?" I asked in a dark whisper.

"What word?" She raised her voice. "**SLUT!?**"

"*Iyana!*" I snapped, but she kept right on rolling.

"Because that's what it looks like I am. You have me strutting around the office like your little plaything, wearing clothes that make me look like a joke."

I bit my tongue, if only to keep from cussing her out and reminding her that she's never once complained about the clothes until now. So what they're part of my fantasy? I own the Tower. There are perks to being the boss—and there are cons to being my captive. That means wearing whatever the heck I want her to wear. Like it or not.

I didn't say any of this, of course, because that would have broken things beyond repair. Instead, I sat quietly as Iyana continued to chew me out. She really laid it on heavy, reminding me that she was a respectable woman until I came along. I took the insults in stride, letting her scream out her frustrations.

She finished with a huff. "You probably need to get your preferences checked out with a psychologist or something." Then she scooted away from me in the car.

I slammed my back against the seat, trying to calm myself.

I didn't want to acknowledge that I might have a slut fantasy, but I didn't need her shouting about it when we got home.

I grunted and leaned over. "Listen, just get through today, and tomorrow I'll take you to get whatever clothes you want. Just don't say you dressed this way for me. And don't say that I have…" I paused, trying not to say it, but Iyana folded her arms and spat it at me, "A slut fantasy?"

"Stop it."

She turned her head.

"Alright!" I almost hollered. I caught Henry eyeing us, and I leaned even closer to Iyana, "I may have a … *dirty* fantasy, alright? I admit it. Is that what you want to hear?"

She didn't respond.

I scooted closer, my breath on her neck as I said, "You're a beautiful woman, Iyana. I like to see you in clothes that show off your figure." My hand went to her knee, sliding up slowly. "Like your hips and your thighs, and I love your—"

"*Alright,*" she snapped her head toward me and swatted at my hands. "I won't say anything. But first thing tomorrow, I want new clothes."

I exhaled, relieved that she would agree so easily.

"Thank you," I said, sitting back against the seats.

The rest of the drive went in silence. Even though I should've taken the time to explain to Iyana what this war was all about, I couldn't bring myself to say anything more to her. It was true, I was bringing her home to see my parents, but I was only doing it to protect her… at least, that's what I kept telling myself.

The car pulled around the cul-de-sac and stopped in front of the only house there. It was in fact a mansion; one my father had built just before he passed BT off to me. I never got to see it finished, but it's as beautiful as I expected it to be.

"Mr. Ortega, and," Henry paused as we stepped out, glancing over at Iyana.

"Miss Walters," I said.

He nodded.

"... And Miss Walters, I welcome you to the Ortega Mansion."

"Thanks, Henry. Just bring our bags in later."

"Of course, sir."

Henry stepped back to the car as we started up the steps. The fountain at the front spouted water, and there were seven statues of dogs drinking around it. There was an empty spot between the dogs, where one more would be placed—it would be my dog. Each one wore a collar with the name of the person who served as head of the Woof Pack. In another ten or twenty years, I'd have a dog constructed for me too, and it'd be drinking right along with the others.

Iyana took each step shakily, with deep breaths and muttering to herself. I grabbed her hand to stop her just before we got to the top.

"It's just my family," I shrugged, "you don't have to be nervous."

She sighed. "What am I supposed to be?" Challa stood on the stairs beside us, sniffing intently along the concrete.

"You're supposed to be you, Iyana. They can be friendly

most times," I said. "The gang life may have been tough, and it might have hardened them a little, but my parents are relatively nice. I think."

"You *think?*"

Nervously, I lifted a shoulder. "I haven't been home in six years. I'm just assuming they haven't changed."

"I can't do this." She let go of my hand and tried to run down the stairs with Challa at her side, but I skipped a few and beat her before she could reach the bottom.

"Iyana, please," I almost whined, "I need you to do this with me."

"Why?" she snapped. "They're *your* parents."

"Because you mean something to me," I said calmly.

Her mouth dropped open, but nothing came out. Only the sound of bickering locusts called out around us.

"Oh," she finally said.

"Having you here will help me keep my head on straight," I admitted weakly.

I didn't know when it'd happened, when I started depending on Iyana, when she became my anchor, but now I knew I would certainly drift away if I didn't have her by my side.

She took a deep breath and reached for my hand. Interlocking her fingers with mine, she climbed up the stairs.

"Okay," she whispered. "I'll go."

I eyed her once more before we started again to the door. When we reached the top, I knocked on it, and my father, a husky pale-skinned man with a salt and pepper beard, opened the door.

"Cortez?"

"Hey, Dad," I said weakly. "I'm home."

11

I Don't Like Her

"Cortez, what are you doing here?" the pale older man asked. He looked like Santa gone rogue, with the matching salt and pepper hair and beard, dark brows, and his wide muscular arms covered in dark tattoos. An inch or so taller than Vito, this man looked like he could pummel Vito, even if he brought a gun to the fight.

"I need your help, Dad," Vito's voice was low and still, like he'd somehow reverted to the Vito I knew when I was first taken in.

Dad... the word echoed until I realized this was Mr. Gerardo—the man who was the head of Woof Pack before Vito.

"Get inside," he said, pulling us into the house. He closed the doors and then leaned against them, eyeing Vito fiercely before flinging his arms open. "Why are you back, out of nowhere?"

"I just told you, I need help, Dad," Vito said.

Mr. Gerardo noticed me for the first time, eyes widening. He blinked at Vito. "Who is she?"

"This is Iyana, she's my—"

"Wife?"

"Secretary," he corrected.

"Why'd you bring your secretary? What happened to Brandon?"

The air became stale, and no one moved.

Mr. Gerardo stiffened, his deep voice coming out low and slow. "What happened to him?"

"Dad," Vito started but a feminine voice called over our shoulders, "Honey? Who's at the door?"

"Not a word to your mother," Mr. Gerardo said, stepping between Vito and me. "Darling, come look!"

A woman rounded the corner, bearing identical features to Vito. Thick dark hair, tan skin, brown eyes, and full lashes. She was as beautiful as Vito was handsome. He looked nothing like Mr. Gerardo, even though he kept calling him 'Dad.' Vito was an exact copy of the woman before us.

"Cortez," she whispered, then she gasped and screamed, "Cortez!" In a blur, she ran down the hall, slamming into Vito's chest. He hugged the small woman, lifting her off her feet. Vito smiled genuinely, as if he'd never been a gang leader who'd murdered someone in cold blood.

"Hey, Mom," he said into her hair. "I missed you."

She was whimpering when she stepped away, tears rolling down her cheeks. While Mr. Gerardo looked like bad Santa, Mrs. Gerardo didn't look like Mrs. Claus, she didn't even look a day over forty.

"Cortez, I can't believe you're home, *hijo*."

"I know." He smiled at her.

"*Mi amor!* Did you come to stay?" the words rolled off her tongue, and even though I couldn't understand much of what she'd said because of her accent, her voice and the rhythm she'd spoken sounded beautiful.

"No," Vito said sadly. "*We're* just visiting."

For the first time, Mrs. Gerardo pulled her eyes from her son, and blinked at me. It hadn't dawned on me that his mother had only asked about *his* stay, but Vito's emphasis got my attention. In fact, she hadn't acknowledged me at all until now. Mr. Gerardo hadn't noticed me either when we first got here, but I didn't think it was for the same reason as Vito's mother with the way she was looking at me now.

"*Quienes ella?*"

"*En ingles, Mama*," Vito responded.

I had no idea he was bilingual. His Spanish was so smooth and fluent, like he spoke it every day.

"Who is she?" his mother repeated.

He slipped a hand behind my back. "She's my secretary."

I smiled shyly and offered my hand. "Hi, I'm Iyana Walters."

Mrs. Gerardo stared at me. For a moment, I thought I'd done something wrong, then she looked back at Vito—back at me again—and chuckled.

"It's so very nice to meet you," she said, taking my hand. "Why don't you two get settled in? Your father and I will get dinner ready."

"Sounds good." Vito eyed his father before shuffling me along.

"Do you want to stay in my room? I'll stay in the guest room," Vito said as we reached the top of the stairs.

"I didn't know you could speak Spanish," I said without thinking.

Vito looked confused, his brows meeting briefly before surrendering to a nod. "Yeah, I speak seven languages, actually. It's good for business."

He opened his door and I glanced at him before stepping inside. "Why is everyone acting funny?"

"No one's acting like anything." He brushed by me.

"Vito," I called firmly, "I don't want to be left out."

He turned to look at me, shreds of worry moving across his face. "Iyana, I'm not leaving you out."

"Then why does it feel like everyone's walking on eggshells around me? Why does it feel like I'm the only one left out on a secret conversation you're all having?"

Vito glanced at the door and moved to close it. "Iyana, sit down."

He gestured toward the bed, but I refused. "No, don't try to smooth me over. You didn't tell me we were coming to visit your parents. You didn't tell me that you knew seven different languages. You don't tell me anything, Vito, and I don't like it."

"I'm protecting you. There are things I don't want to tell you because I can take care of it. Because I don't need you worrying about me."

"I'm always worried about you!"

I couldn't breathe because the truth had winded me. Vito had slowly become important to me, and there wasn't a day that went by where I wasn't worrying about him when he wasn't in the Tower.

"The war, I'm trying to keep it political and bloodless. All that means is taking businesses, which I can manage for the most part, but if things get out of hand, I'm going to need a backup plan. And I need to make sure all my connections are set to back me if I'm forced to make drastic decisions." His eyes hit the floor in the silence, and my heart finally began to slow down.

"Why couldn't you just tell me that?"

"Because I'm trying to protect you. You don't need to know the ins and outs, and I don't want you to."

"Why not?"

"Because if you knew the truth, how this war is only bloodless because of the pile of bodies I created over these last six years, you wouldn't look at me the same. The way I've ended lives for my own benefit, the way it didn't always mean something to squeeze the trigger."

"Vito..." I crossed the room to him, "you're not like that anymore."

"Yes, I am," he snapped.

"*No*, you aren't." I placed a hand on his chin and lifted his head to see his eyes. "If you were the same, you wouldn't be here doing everything you can to keep people from dying in this war."

"Cortez! Iyana! Dinner is almost ready!" His father called loudly.

Vito gave me a half-smile, his dark eyes almost brightened as he said, "We better get down there." He took me by the hand and led me out the room.

At the table, Mr. Gerardo sat at one end with Mrs. Gerardo at the other end. "Sit across from each other," his mother requested.

I smiled and nodded as I took a seat across from Vito.

"So, Cortez, how's everything going with the business?" his mother asked as she forked a dark piece of broccoli.

"It's going good, Mom. We're making some good decisions."

"Good." She smiled.

Vito glanced over at me, and I gave him a warm smile, hoping he knew that I understood to keep quiet about BT.

"Dafni, sweetheart, why don't you introduce yourself?" Mr. Gerardo suggested as he cut into his steak.

"For what?" She looked up from her meal, and Mr. Gerardo shot his eyes at me.

"For her? Please." She waved a hand. "She's lucky to be here."

"Don't talk about Iyana like that," Vito said. "She has a

name."

"A very ugly one."

"It's a whole lot better than Dafni," I said.

Everyone's forks stopped at once, and all eyes fell on me. But I was only concerned with Vito's. A corner of his mouth raised into a smile, and he looked back at his mother, "What were you saying?"

"How dare you bring such a disrespectful woman to our home? I don't like her! Get her out of my house! *Ahora!*"

"*No*," Vito snapped. "She hasn't done anything wrong. You're always like this when it comes to women I like. When is it going to end?"

"You *like* her? Please, Cortez, look at her! *Ella no es nada!*"

"*Stop* it." Vito glanced at me and then at his father. "If you're going to talk about Iyana, at least do it in English so she can defend herself."

"No." Dafni shook her head.

"Yes, or we're leaving." His voice was low and threatening—his mother tightened her jaw in response. She cast me a look of utter disgust and discontent. I casually looked to Vito, but it was his father's voice that called all our attention.

Sitting opposite of his wife, Mr. Gerardo set down his fork and knife and said, "Are you two done? Our guest speaks English, Dafni. I'm not going to say that again."

Dafni cowered, slumping her shoulders as she dropped her eyes from her husband's to her plate of roasted duck.

Mr. Gerado's gaze landed on me. "Now, Iyana, I'm sorry these two were arguing, we aren't usually like this. I know tensions are high right now, but is there anything you'd like to add? Anything you want to say to defend yourself?"

"No," I said softly.

"You sure? Because I want to move on with dinner, but it wouldn't be fair if you didn't get to speak your mind."

"No, Mr. Gerardo, I don't have anything to add."

"Very well." He focused back on Dafni, giving her a look of agitation before he said to his son, "How was the flight, Vito?"

"It was alright," he said flatly.

"Oh, come on." Mr. Gerardo showed his teeth through the gateway of his beard. "Don't tell me your mother ruined the mood?"

Dafni tsked. "It was that wretched woman you brought here." She turned and smirked at me. "Do you get it now that it's in your language?"

"Mom—"

"Vito," I said hotly, "I've got this."

He swallowed loudly and I turned to his mother. "I don't speak much Spanish, but I understood enough to piece together that you said I was nothing. You took one look at me and judged me, and your judgement is way off. But you wouldn't know that." I shook my head. "You never even considered why Vito would bring his secretary across the country with him if she wasn't important, knowing he had to face you."

Dafni's smirk dropped quickly into a frown but before she could hurl another nasty remark, I said, "I've done nothing but help Vito and his business—which you know nothing about." I stood from the table and tossed my napkin on the plate. "Thanks for the food, but I'm not hungry."

"Wait," Dafni snapped before Vito could, "it takes a lot of guts to stand up to me."

"That shouldn't be something you pride yourself on," I seethed before I left the dining room.

"Iyana, wait up!" I heard Vito calling after me.

I burst into the bedroom and stood in the middle of the floor, covering my mouth. I'd never snapped on anyone like that before.

"Iyana," Vito called as he rushed into the room. "I'm so sorry. If you want to go home, we can. I'll get help another way."

I shook my head, sighing. "No. I know you need to be here. And I'm sorry, I shouldn't have said those things to your mother."

Vito shrugged. "My mom gets vicious sometimes. My parents are usually nice, but Mom's a little rough around the edges when it comes to women."

"It's alright." I sat on the bed, and he reached for my hand.

"You must be really upset," he said with a smirk. "You didn't even ask about the women I've brought home."

I chuckled. I hadn't noticed that he'd mentioned other women. "I'm not upset, I just feel bad for snapping like that and making things worse between us."

"She'll ease up." He shrugged. "Don't even worry about it."

I gave him a harrumph. "Seems like you've brought enough women here to make things difficult with her."

He laughed. "*Now* you're interested in the other women?"

"I just want to know what could've happened between your exes and your mother for her to be so vicious right off the bat."

He leaned forward and kissed my forehead. "I promise I'm not keeping you out of the loop when I tell you that my mother has *always* been that way."

"Really?" I muttered as he stood.

Tired eyes seemed to sigh with relief as he walked to the door. "Yeah." He nodded. "Listen, Ana, if you can deal with her for a few more days, I promise to start telling you more. I promise I'll keep you in the loop from now on."

"I can do that," I said slowly.

"Good." He sighed in relief.

"I think I'm going to retire for the night."

"Alright, the shower's through there." He pointed to a white door in his plain and mostly empty room. "I'll see you in the morning."

"Goodnight, Vito."

"Goodnight, Iyana."

12

Advice

I took my time getting out of bed today. I didn't exactly feel like walking the streets of LA to find Iyana some new clothes, I needed to take care of business. I needed to have an important conversation with my father. But I made a promise to her, and she took a bullet last night from my mother. Iyana handled herself really well; I'm beginning to think I've underestimated her strength.

    I came down the stairs thinking of what Iyana's personal style might be. When I met her, she was wearing slacks, sneakers, and a button-down shirt. She didn't exactly look bad, she just looked plain. Although, her plain look was still relatively attractive, I never expected her to look as stunning as she did every day in the clothes Jewels picked out for her. Jewels and I may have our differences, but I am grateful for what she's done with Iyana.

"Cortez…"

I looked up and found my father sitting at the head of the dining room table. He was the only person in the room, reading a newspaper and drinking strong coffee.

"Morning, Dad," I said, sinking my hands into my pockets. "Have you seen Iyana?"

He turned a page in his newspaper. "I had your mother take her out shopping."

"Mom? Why?"

He closed his newspaper and set it on the table. My father was a kind man, but when he needed to be stern, it was his agonizing silence that dealt the most damage. He'd make me sit in silence when I was younger. It'd be so quiet, I swore I could hear the closing and opening of each synapse in his body.

I hated the silence because my father wouldn't move from his seat at the head of the table. He'd just watch me, making me think of all the ways I could kill myself after he finished staring me down for what seemed like hours. He told me one time that silence was a time to reflect, to come up with an answer that wouldn't get me pummeled by him. Around the age of sixteen, I'd become a master of the silence, manipulating my father with self-made confidence to back every decision I made, and a good explanation on why my poor choice could become an opportunity somehow.

It wasn't until I took over BT that I appreciated my father's training. Being able to make tough decisions and feel nothing but security in my own choices was valuable. How could anyone follow the leader if you weren't firm in your decisions, good or bad?

Today was no different. It was a test to see if all his training had paid off. I swallowed thickly, and began, "Dad, I—"

"You need to tell me why this girl is here and what's really going on with the Pack."

"May I sit?"

He nodded. "You may."

I crossed the room and sat at the table beside him.

"Let's start with your secretary. Where did she come from?"

Silence echoed. My father hated strays, he usually killed them, but there were a few times he didn't, like in Jewels' case.

"She was… she was picked up."

His brow raised, and a tick of annoyance crept in. "Picked up from the bus stop? Picked up on your way over here as a hooker? I don't know what you're talking about, Cortez."

"She was caught in the crossfire, and we took her in," I said without looking at him.

"You brought a woman you barely know into my house? Do you know what she could do to this family?"

"Dad, it's not like that."

"Cortez, you don't know her! You've put everyone in danger! Everything I've built—"

"She's not like that!" I snapped.

My father flinched, his eyes scurrying over me in an instant.

"Iyana isn't like that," I repeated after taking a breath. "She's different. We're not in danger with her. You know I wouldn't do that to us. I've spent the last six years protecting you and Mom, cleaning up the messes you made, and you're accusing me of bringing our family down?" I sat back in my chair, scowling fiercely at my father.

He nodded, dropping his shoulders. "I didn't mean it like that, and you know it." He paused, tapping his fingers on the table. "Give me some security in knowing she's trustworthy."

"After everything I just said?"

"Sleeping with a woman like that can mess with your head."

I forgot I was the only one who started going to church six years ago. I doubt my father would ever believe I've kept my virtue after Jewels, but it wasn't the time to explain that now.

Pathetically, I said, "I'm not sleeping with her. We haven't slept together at all since she's been here."

"How long is that?"

"Six months."

"Then, who have you been sleeping with, and why didn't you bring her?"

"I haven't been sleeping with anyone."

My dad looked worried for a second, like there could be something wrong with me for not sleeping with Iyana.

"Cortez, you're not sick or changing sides, are you?"

"Did you just ask if I'm gay?"

He shrugged. "You've always been a little soft on the inside. I didn't do a good job beating that out of you."

"Dad?" I said, bewildered.

"Alright." He waved his hands. "So, if none of those apply,

then what's the hold up? Iyana's a beautiful girl. And if not her then why no one at all?"

"It's not," I paused. I didn't want to say it out loud, but I couldn't keep it to myself since my lacking sex life equated to homosexuality or an STD in my father's head, "it's not like I don't *want* to sleep with her."

My father chuckled. "I know. Watching her prance around that place in clothes like that, I know you're thinking about her every night." He raised a brow with a smirk on his face and I couldn't keep myself from smiling too. The number of times I've left my bedroom and stood at my loft's door, wondering how it'd look to everyone if I went to Iyana's place through the night, was too many to count.

"That's not the point," I said. "The point is that she can be trusted."

"Give me some proof."

"We had an incident at a store."

"I heard about that."

Leave it to my father to keep tabs on the Pack while living halfway across the country.

"Yeah, it was a run in with Gang Grizzly."

His eyes narrowed, but he didn't know half the problems I was having yet—tabs or not.

"She had the chance to run," I continued. "I got shot, and everyone deserted me except her."

"Where was Brandon?"

I shrugged. "Helping someone else. But she came and got me out of there. Patched me up and stayed by my side."

"She stayed behind instead of taking her chance to go home?"

I nodded.

"Did she know that BT and all your clients would come after her?"

"She did. I thought the same thing, that she only stayed for her safety, but she told me something three months ago. She said she didn't *want* to go home, she wanted to stay with me at BT."

His brows lifted and fell quickly before he folded his arms and eyed me for a moment. "I see. So, she likes you?"

"Yeah, I think so," I said as thoughts of Iyana and I sharing her couch flashed in my head. Remembering her made me feel things I tried not to, at least in front of my father, because I could feel a stupid grin trying to work its way onto my face.

"But that's not the problem, is it?" He paused. "You like her, don't you?"

I took a breath because what I was going to say next was outrageous, but somewhere inside, I knew it was the truth I couldn't run from anymore.

"Dad, I think it's worse than that." I paused. "I think I love her."

No words were spoken for at least fifteen seconds. It was just my father thinking and breathing before he said, "When I saw you yesterday, you looked different. I knew something was up when you defended her at dinner and told your mother to speak English around her. I didn't know that my son had finally become a man."

My eyes shot to him in pure shock. I was expecting to be beaten until I came to the senses of my father. But instead, he was holding a half smile on his face, and nodding in approval.

"What?" was all I managed.

"You're a man now, Cortez, you've found someone to love, and you came here to tell me you want to get out of BT, right?"

I shook my head. "No. I came back because a gang war has started. I need help."

"A gang war? How?"

I sighed. "We had a rat, and that rat was working with Grizzly," I stammered, "*is* working with Grizzly?"

"'*Is*' as in 'is still alive'?"

"Yeah."

He watched me for a second. "Who was it?"

I hesitated, and my father began to look worried. If it had been some lower level, he wouldn't have cared. But a name, one that I didn't want to say, made my father realize the weight of the situation.

If I remembered your name, that meant you knew secrets, you played an integral role at BT. But if my father could remember your name, then BT was just as much your responsibility as mine or his.

"It was, uh," my voice fell flat. "Brandon."

He flinched away, like there was no way this could be true. Unfortunately, it was.

"Brandon? Are you sure?"

"I brought some information with me, just so you can look

it over."

He scooted back from the table and stood. I watched him pace the floor. If too much of BT's information got to Grizzly, my father and mother could be in danger. Grizzly might just pay a visit to my father just to scare me, or to shake me. That's why I needed serious help.

"Who started it?"

"One of my guys were fighting, and he shot someone."

My father almost lost his breath. "Cortez…"

"I know," I said, shrugging, "but I need help."

"How can I help you? Brandon has everything!"

"That's why I need to outsmart him, Dad. He's going to take all those legendary accounts and BT will be nothing. He could even tell Grizzly where you live since you left him that information despite my warning against it."

He collapsed in his chair, visibly shaken and paling. "You've got to beat him at his own game."

"How?"

"You need to secure more accounts. Enough to cover your legendary accounts in case he takes them."

"Dad, that's millions of dollars. Where can I get that from?"

"You need to flush some money into BT, give it some padding. Pour a little into your brothel and start another service. You need to acquire favors—make it so that people owe you."

"So, go back to grunt work?"

"On a bigger scale. Call your best guy and tell him to host

a party for BT. The best thing you can do is prepare to lose your biggest accounts."

I groaned. I'd hoped that wouldn't be his suggestion but, somehow, I knew it was the only way.

He stood from the table, rubbing his forehead. "So, ask the question you really want to ask me." He started out the dining room for his office and I followed him.

"I don't know what you mean."

"Come on," he said as he walked inside, "ask me how to protect Iyana."

I froze in the doorway.

"It's why you brought her here. You were scared someone might attack the Tower, and you didn't want her there."

"Yeah," I said, stepping inside.

Nothing had changed about my father's office. Big brown chairs, a beige rug, blank walls, and a big, long desk.

"You want to protect her? Stop hiding her." He used a key to open a drawer on his desk. He pulled out rolls of money, a pipe, tabaco, his silver tamper with BT engraved into it, and a pack of matches.

"What do you mean?"

Dad sat down in his chair and began stuffing his pipe. Pinch by pinch, he added tobacco to his pipe and patted it with his tamper.

"I mean, stop trying to protect her. Put her out in public, allow them to put a target on her head. No one will kill someone who doesn't matter to you."

"I can't do that," I said as I watched him strike his match.

He watched it burn for a few seconds until the red head was gone and the fire inched down the match. Ringing his pipe, he lit it once, and then again before putting it out.

"I've never been in a gang war, but I've come close enough to them to know that wars may start out political, but hardly do they stay that way. You need to put her in a position where she's not going to be seen as your weakness. If, for a second, they think you like her more than any other person you have working for you, they'll take her."

"I know," I said hotly, "but what does that have to do with letting a target be on her head?"

"Putting a target on her head means she's up for grabs. Means she's not important."

"But Brandon already has an idea that I might like her."

He took a puff on his pipe, lifting dark eyes to mine. "Then you only have one choice left."

"What's that?"

He pulled his pipe from his lips. "Marry her."

13

The One Who Started It All

"We are going to visit as many stores as possible," Dafni said.

I gave her a small smile and looked out the window. The plan was to have Vito take me, but this morning I was awakened by his mother and asked to spend the day shopping with her. She wanted to make up for last night. It was alright, considering Vito and I had already planned to shop, but somehow, it was less exciting with his mother as his replacement, especially since she didn't like me.

"I know I was harsh last night," she said. "But that was only because I wanted to see what you were made of. I needed to see what my son sees in you."

"Excuse me?"

She glanced away from the road to look me over. "My son, he seems to really like you. He's never been so serious with a woman before, serious enough to ask me to respect her."

"Why would you blatantly disrespect someone just because they're with Vito?"

She cackled. "Because I know my son's worth, and the usual women clinging to his arm are just whores who want his money."

"Then that should've been a conversation between you and him. You don't have to treat someone poorly even if they have impure motives. And you don't know everyone, there are genuine people who sincerely care about Vito."

"But I bet you're glad I chased them away. Now's your chance to have my son."

I stared at the side of her face, wondering why she was so evil. "You're a horrible person," I said, and she smiled.

"You are gutsy, saying that to someone's mother."

"I think it's gutsy of you to assume that I would cower to your indirect threats."

"What?" she said dramatically as we slowed for a red light. "I promise I'm not—"

"Vito loves you," I cut her off, "and he expects you to respect me. Not treat me like this."

She cleared her throat and pulled off at the green light. "I know," she said quietly, "I just don't want to lose him." Her voice trembled as she drove. "When Gerardo was working all the time, it was Cortez who took care of me, protected me. We were so close, and I couldn't bear anyone getting close to him. And when I saw the way he looked at you..." she shook her head. "It was supposed to make me happy that Cortez had fallen in love, not angry. But I was so mad, furious even. Because I was losing the only person I thought I never would."

"Love me?" I couldn't get past that. "Vito doesn't love me," I said mostly to myself.

"Oh please." She wiped at her tears. "He loves you and you love him. Both of you are just too shy to say something. You guys reek of love."

"No." I shook my head. "That can't be true." I pushed back into the seat, trying to get the sudden tension knot out of my neck.

"You're not a secretary. You're his love interest."

I shook my head, trying to deny what seemed so obvious. But that couldn't be true. Vito and I worked together, we'd gotten close, and we'd even made out once, but that was by all accounts lust, *not* love.

"When I met Tobias Gerardo, I thought I'd never love anyone again, until I had Cortez. Gerardo became distant with his work, and Cortez and I became close. But there'd be times when he'd meet someone, and he'd bring her home, wanting the only person he cared about to meet the person he was interested in." She hiccupped. "I was too selfish to see that, in some way, that was actually Cortez's way of telling me he loved me."

"I don't understand though," I said as we pulled into a parking space. "Mr. Gerardo is here now, all the time. Why don't you spend time with him?"

"We try, but Gerardo and I had drifted so far apart, it's been hard piecing our relationship back together. The first three years after Cortez left, we barely spoke. He had different women every night, and I usually left to find someone for myself. I just," she paused as she put the car in park, "I couldn't forgive Gerardo for sending my son off. I know that he was working in a bad business, I don't know everything, but I know it was bad enough to scare him into a corner and take our only son and give him away. He sent him to cover for him, changed his name and nearly erased everything about Cortez."

She covered her face as she began to sob.

"He gave our boy to the streets and never even tried to help him! He let my son go, my only child, and there was nothing I could do because I was the reason he did it. I didn't listen when he told me not to go someplace, and I was taken, beaten, nearly killed."

I watched in horror as I realized the woman I thought was just bitter was actually broken.

"It's my fault Cortez was forced to take over his father's business. Cortez's real father asked me to meet him somewhere, and I went, against Gerardo's wishes. Fernando, Cortez's father, was working with some bad business who wanted Gerardo." Her tears were still falling, but she'd calmed down as she sat in the driver's seat, recalling the dark times surrounding Vito's rise to the head of BT.

"I was still in love with Fernando. I'd been seeing him while married to Gerardo. I'd only left him because he was abusive. But when I got pregnant by him, I finally told Gerardo. Eventually, things worked themselves out. We raised Cortez, and when he was about eighteen, Fernando came up again, and I fell for his trap."

"You started seeing him again?"

She nodded, and finally looked over at me. Black liner stained her cheeks as she heaved a great sniffle. "I'm stupid, I know. Cortez had started going to church and was being consumed by that. He'd brought home two different women over those two years, both were very good girls, but I was jealous. That's what fueled my affair. The two men I loved seemed to be interested in everything but me."

"So you went back to Fernando, and he finally tricked you and lured Gerardo out."

She nodded quickly, and her breathing picked up. She was trying not to cry, but it was an overwhelming story, one where she sat in the middle of it.

"The only way out of this mess was to bring Cortez into it. He doesn't know the whole truth. Gerardo didn't want him to know that I was the reason for all of our problems." She shook her head, brown wavy hair shimmied around her as she tried to hold in her sobs. "He killed Fernando, but in return, offered Cortez to keep more problems from arising."

"No," I whispered, "he was keeping a war from breaking out."

I sighed as I looked out the window. Vito was the peace offering. Giving up Vito was Gerardo's way of losing everything, and that was acceptable for whatever gang he was warring with back then.

"What?" She called my attention back to her confused eyes.

"Oh," I shook my head, "nothing."

"You know more about this work than I do." She grabbed my hand. "Please tell me the truth. What is Cortez involved in?"

I read her eyes, pained with guilt and shame, but even so, I remembered Mr. Gerardo's firm words, *not a word of this to your mother,* or in my case, to Dafni.

"I'm sorry, Dafni, I can't tell you."

"Why not?" she pleaded.

I chewed my lip and echoed the words I'd been living by for the past six months, "The less you know, the better off you are."

"That's not right! I deserve the truth," she snapped.

"And what about Vito? Don't you think he deserves to know the truth? He deserves to know that your selfishness pulled him out of a perfect world and into the lifestyle he's stuck in?"

Her mouth hung open before she closed it to swallow loudly. "He will hate me," she whispered.

I couldn't pity her, considering this whole ordeal was her fault and it didn't have to be this way. "He'll hate you more if he finds out from me."

She began to pout, and tears swelled in her eyes, but before she could say anything, I stopped her. "I'm not going to tell him yet; I don't think he needs to know right now. But when things are better for us, then you'll have a chance to tell him, and if you don't, I will."

"Us," she whispered. "You are already thinking of yourself

as part of his family."

I couldn't refute her because I didn't know if what she said was true. I thought I only meant BT when I'd said 'us,' but somewhere inside me, I knew I meant Vito and me.

Dafni sniffled. "I will tell him. You call me when things are better, and I will tell him."

14

Visiting Hours

"Welcome to Saint Sessa's Hospital. Are you checking in or visiting?" A woman with too much makeup and bright red lips spoke chirpily at me.

"Just visiting."

"Alright, I'll need the patient's name and your ID."

I pulled my wallet out and dug through it. "I'm here to see Velma Walters."

Red painted fingers took my ID and began typing things into her computer. "She's got more community visitors lately. Are you from the community?"

"No," I said flatly. "I'm a close friend of the family. Her husband's friend, actually."

"Oh, well you're in for a treat." She smiled widely, bearing all her large white teeth at me. "Mr. Walters is upstairs. He's the only one checked in today and has not checked out."

"Perfect," I said as she slid me the ID.

"Alright, you are all set."

"Thank you."

I nodded as I left the desk and headed for the elevators. As I rode up, I checked my phone, reading through old texts from Tim and me. When I got off the elevator, I waved to a few nurses and made my way down the hall to Velma's room. Tim was at her bedside, whispering to her.

"Timothy," I said loudly.

He jerked at his name and turned to see me. "Brandon? What are you doing here?"

"Am I not allowed to see your wife now?" I came over and sat beside him and looked over at Velma. Her chest rose and fell steadily as the humming of the machines made the whole room sound like one big vibration. "How is she?"

"You know how she is," Tim snapped.

"Ouch," I teased, "you seem bitter, Mr. Walters."

"You need to stop this, Brandon."

"You need to give me my money," I said, looking over at him. "Oh, but I forgot, you can't. Because every dime you have acquired over the past five years has been off my back."

"That's not true," he growled.

"Then you tell me how things are working around here. You tell me who's been footing your hospital bills for the last five years. Who helped you when you came running to them for money?"

"I thought you were my friend," he said quietly.

"I was, and I still am. That's why I never asked for the money back initially."

"No," he snapped, "you didn't ask because you knew I'd need more until I owed you too much to pay back and now I'm stuck! I'm stuck in this never-ending cycle of doing tasks for you, and I just," his voice cracked, "I just want to be done."

I crossed my legs and smirked at him. "That's what happens when you make a deal with the devil isn't it? You get in, you get what you want but when it becomes too much or you're tired, then you want to jump out." I shrugged. "It doesn't work that way."

"This is all a game to you, isn't it?" He tried to sound angry, but he only sounded weak and pathetic.

"Whatever it is to me shouldn't concern you. You just need to be ready for the next task I give you."

"No," he said angrily. "I'm not doing anything else for you. I'm going to the police after this and telling them everything. I don't care if I go to prison. I've already lost everything. I just want my wife to wake up." I nodded as I listened to him ramble. When he finished his great plan, I said, "My guys on the force would never let your accusations make it past the front desk. So, make your threats a little stronger next time."

"You've screwed me!" he shouted.

"No, Timothy, *you* screwed *me*!" I stood to my feet abruptly. "You screwed me twice already. Iyana was a fluke! The girl knew nothing about the Abeltons after I convinced Vito to invade their home. I knew they wouldn't be there. I knew we weren't going to catch them. But I trusted your word that Iyana knew the Abletons because she'd been sitting for them." I took a breath and tried to calm myself. "After all the funding I poured into your community projects, all the money I spend keeping your wife alive, I thought you'd be more appreciative."

"You're keeping her sedated! You're keeping her in this medically induced coma, running up your own bill!"

I unbuttoned the first button on my purple shirt and breathed deeply. "You haven't given me anything to work with, Tim." I took my seat again. "Five years ago, when you were flat broke, swamped in debt, I came and donated to you. It was a large donation that would've taken away a lot of your debt. You had no problem taking my money then. You even came back for me, thinking I was this generous guy who just wanted to see the community's leader get his wife out of the hospital."

"How wrong I was," he said as he scowled.

"Oh please." I waved a hand. "Did you forget the part where you came back to the person who donated a lot and asked for more? Did you think that wouldn't come with a price tag?"

"What is wrong with you? You could've just said 'no.'"

"But you were weak, and I needed that. You needed me, and things seem to have worked themselves out."

"No, they haven't. You're keeping my wife medicated so that she'll stay in this state of limbo. Never moving. Never speaking. While you go off and enjoy your life, I'm here praying for a solution."

"Seems to me like you might need to pray a little harder.

Don't think He hears you."

"Why are you here?" he snapped.

"I told you," I shrugged, "I came to see Velma, and I came to see you."

He stared, his wide nostrils flared, and his eyes lowered, he looked angrier than a brahma bull.

"There's no need to thank me," I said after a moment of silence between us. I pulled out a ticket and handed it to him. "I got you a spot on a very important dinner party coming up. You are officially running for mayor of New York City, and you will be making an important speech on community outreach. I'll have some guys there working the crowd to back you, and I will be there too."

He sat there blinking at the ticket in his hand. "I can't run for mayor. I… I won't run. I won't do it."

"Yes, you can," I said firmly, "and yes you will. Now, I've got to go, but you make sure you're early to this event. I wouldn't want you to miss the gatherers before the event begins."

"And if I don't show?"

"It'll be because you were killed," I said as I stood and buttoned my suit jacket. "You have no reason to miss this engagement." I leaned down close and whispered, "If you do, for whatever reason, I will kill Iyana, and drag her dead corpse here and wake your wife up to see it. Then I'll kill her too." I stood up straight and winked. "Mayor Timothy Walters. It has a ring to it, doesn't it?"

After the hospital visit, I drove over to Grizzly's place and requested an immediate meeting with him. He hated when I did that, but after all the work I've done for him, I believed I was deserving of a meeting when I needed to see him. It wasn't like Grizzly was ever busy. I did all his errands and made connections while his cubs did all the grunt work. Grizzly spent most of his days in his hot springs, relaxing with women and alcohol. The only time he worked was when it was absolutely necessary, which was almost never.

"Why are you interrupting me, Brandon?" he growled as he sat at his grand desk. The entire thing was carved out of a single tree for his great grandfather, and still holds all the beauty and grandeur as it did all those years ago. Great Grizzly, Grizzly's great grandfather, tried to start up Gang Grizzly some time ago but failed miserably. Grizzly brought that dream to life, and now carries Great Grizzly's cane, uses his furs, and as many things of his that he could find to honor him.

"Because I have some great news."

He raised his head, wrinkly skin sagged into a frown. "What is it?"

"I thought you'd be excited over good news."

"Your good news is never actually good."

"It is today," I said, swinging my hands open. "I've got someone on the ballot to be mayor of New York City."

Grizzly adjusted and I waited in an aching silence, wondering why he wasn't smiling. "I'm assuming this has some correlation with Jersey?"

"Of course," I cleared my throat. "My guy takes the seat as

NYC's mayor, it means Vito's grasp on New York loosens and the prince of the city loses his throne. Which means clients are going to be looking for the next new thing, the next *best* thing, and that's you. You're the only one who's actually a rival to the Woof Pack."

"You think a bunch of New York businesses are going to want to run to Jersey? Think again."

"That's where you're wrong." I stepped closer, and he scowled. I took a step back and said, "These guys, without their prince, will have no suppliers. My guy will be able to point everyone in the right direction *away* from Vito and BT."

Grizzly fell quiet as he leaned back in his chair. He rocked as he thought it over, and then he nodded. "Very good, Brandon."

I released a breath and said, "Grizzly, this is going to change things for the gang. There's an engagement where all the candidates, and a few really popular people, are going to be next week. I'll be going to do some networking. I want to start planting seeds of security while my guy gives a speech."

He nodded. "This is good. My gang will run New York City and all of Jersey." He took a breath and folded his hands on his desk. "Did you secure one of Vito's clients yet for our move in this war?"

"I did." I nodded. "I secured a marijuana account equivalent to a cub. I didn't want to go too high or else he might try to take too much during his retaliation."

"Fair enough. Anything else?"

I shook my head and he stood from his chair. Brown and

black fur sat on his shoulders as he hulked over me. "Good work, Brandon." He turned and gestured at his guard to open the door for him.

"Thank you, Grizzly," I called as he exited the room.

15

The Teacher and The Pet

"Morning, Hardy," Logan said as he walked into Vito's living room.

"Morning," I said.

"You still sulking?" He shoved my feet off the couch and sat down.

"I'm the worst person in the entire Tower."

"Yeah. Brandon was the worst, but since he left, now you're it."

I punched his shoulder. "Shut up, Logan."

He leaned back and checked his watch. Pushing dark hairs out of his face he said, "Jewels is coming up here in a few minutes, and then Kat. I've got to break the news to Jewels about what her involvement with Brandon means for the Tower."

I nodded. "I see."

"And Kat's just coming to tell me about some security updates, nothing major."

"You're telling me all this because you don't want me seeing Jewels anymore, aren't you?"

He adjusted to face me. Chilling eyes fleeted over me behind the ruthless dark hairs that never stayed back no matter how much he pushed them away. "I'm telling you this because you need to be careful. I personally don't think you should see her anymore. You're too young and immature for something like this."

"Logan, you're one year older than me."

"Yeah, but we're different. Sex is sex, I get that. But to you, sex means a relationship. You can't let it go. You become vulnerable and you might tell her things you shouldn't."

I opened my mouth to argue, but there was no use. I was in love with Jewels, but it wasn't because of the sex. I knew we had a connection, and now that Brandon was out of the way, she would take me more seriously.

I sat back against the couch, mulling over what Logan said when a knock came to the door.

"I'll get it," Logan said as he moved from the couch.

My heart began to thud in my chest when Logan opened the door and Jewels' voice came from the hall.

"Hey, Logan," her voice sounded sultry, like she was flirting with him.

"Morning," he said nonchalantly. "Come in."

Slender legs brought her through the door. She was

smiling, glancing back at Logan who was smiling at her. The two shared a silent exchange in that moment, and my heart almost shattered at the thought of Jewels sleeping with Logan, or anyone else for that matter. When her eyes caught mine, she stopped in her tracks, staring blankly at me before her smile changed. It wasn't the same one she'd given to Logan, it was forced and full of shock.

"Hey, Hardy." She stepped down into the living room. "I didn't know you'd be here."

"Fancy that," I said sorely.

She nodded and turned away.

"So, we're not going to talk about this?" I said, standing behind her now.

"There's nothing to talk about." She walked away, leaving me in the living room while she headed to the kitchen where Logan was. "What did you bring me here for?" Jewels asked Logan.

I stood in the hall leading to the kitchen and listened from there. I didn't want to pry, but I couldn't help it, not after the way they interacted when she came in.

"Vito's cutting your hours at the brothel. You're going to be here in the Tower, across from Iyana, with guards at your door twenty-four-seven."

"Excuse me? What is the meaning of this?"

"The rat was Brandon."

I heard her gasp, and for a moment the entire place was silent.

"So, you're all suspicious of me because I slept with the

guy? Who cares!? This is ridiculous and I'm not standing for it."

I heard her footsteps and raced back to the living room. She marched past me to Vito's office with Logan hot on her heels.

"He's not here."

"What, he wasn't man enough to tell me himself?"

"You weren't important enough for him to deliver the news himself," Logan snapped.

"I'm going back to my place and I'm quitting."

"Your things are currently being moved into the apartment across from Iyana's. If you leave this tower without our knowledge—"

"What? Are you going to kill me? Because I'm already dead if I'm being treated like a prisoner!"

"Don't make this difficult," Logan said. "Let me take you to your new place so you can tell the movers where you want certain things."

"Incredible," she said as she thundered through Vito's place.

Logan came out rushing behind her. "When Kat comes up, tell her I'm away and to reschedule."

"How long will it be to take her to her apartment?"

He shrugged as he caught the door Jewels just walked out of. "It might take a while. I'm going to help her out as a testament of good will on our part." He stepped out the door in a rush, pulling it shut behind him.

"He's going to sleep with her," I said aloud.

I sank my head into my hands, trying not to be emotional. I tried to convince myself that she loved me, that she wouldn't do that to me, but I saw the way she looked at him, and the way he looked at her. Before I could drown any further in my thoughts, I heard Kat at the door. When I opened it, she stood there, blue eyes and blonde hair with brown streaks in it.

"Hey, I'm looking for Logan?"

"He's downstairs sleeping with Jewels. And he told me not to sleep with her because I couldn't handle it, but apparently, he can. So, you need to reschedule."

Her eyes widened, and she bit her lip for a moment before she asked, "Do you want to eat lunch with me? I was supposed to have a working lunch, but since Leo's down there, I can eat up here."

Scratching my head, I didn't answer. I didn't have an appetite at all after starting a war and losing the woman I loved within a ninety-six-hour period.

"Do you know if Vito has fresh lemons?" She pushed her way inside and headed to the kitchen. "Fresh lemons are great for making lemon garlic chicken," she called.

I closed the door and made my way to the kitchen where Kat was already taking pans out of the cabinets.

"Look… back there at the door, I don't know what I was saying."

"I was married at your age and fresh meat in the marines."

I squinted. I thought Kat was a lesbian, but I didn't say anything.

"My husband and I went in together straight out of high

school. I loved him," she said as she set out some ingredients from the fridge. "But he cheated on me. I didn't find out for a while and then I tried to kill him and the woman he'd been cheating with for years." She looked up from the knife in her hand. "It was a car accident. I rammed them off the road, just not hard enough to kill them. But it scared the girl, and she ended up leaving him which was good enough for me at the time." She chopped some vegetables in silence, and I took a seat at the bar. I didn't know Kat had gone through all of that, but I never really knew much about her in the first place.

"What happened after that?"

She looked up from the mushrooms she'd been chopping. "I was dishonorably discharged from the marines. Took on a fake identity across the country, in Jersey, but landed a teaching job in the Bronx. I worked there for a few years until I was found out."

"How'd they find out?"

"Someone didn't like me, so they dug up dirt about me. The town I said I was from didn't have any records of a natural disaster for the past thirty years. I'd told the school I'd been working at that my records were lost because of a flood, and that the town was recovering them. They only pestered me for a while, but since the kids loved me, and I had an eighty-percent regents passing score with my students getting a seventy-five or higher, they let it go."

"Someone always gets jealous." I sighed.

She laughed as she dumped all her ingredients into a bowl and began to shave some lemon over it. "They do." She nodded. "But it all ended up working out, because I wound up here."

"You got taken in by a gang," I said. "How is that good?"

"I got saved because of this gang, and accepting Christ is the best decision I've made in my entire life."

"Christ? I've heard Iyana talking about Him."

She was seasoning the chicken now, turning it over and rubbing in the herbs. "I'm glad she's mentioned Him to you. You should think about talking to Him."

"You mean praying?"

She smiled without looking up at me.

"I guess I'd better, since you're the second person to tell me to talk to Him."

"God's tugging at your heart, you should answer."

"I'll consider it."

"Fair enough," she said, turning on the skillet.

16

From a Princess to a King

When we arrived back to the Gerardo's, Challa rounded the corner and laid down for a belly rub.

"Hi Challa-Walla," I said as I rubbed his belly. He squirmed on the floor in excitement before rolling over and licking my hand.

"We're home!" Dafni said as she came in behind me. Two men walked in with our things, and she stopped them. "Have my bags taken to my room. Iyana's should go to hers."

"Of course." One of the men nodded before taking our things upstairs.

I fiddled my hands nervously as I decided to put on one of the outfits I bought at Dafni's request. She'd been nicer since we talked in the car, and I was actually beginning to take a liking to her. Vito was right, she eventually eased up and is surprisingly funny.

"Don't worry," she said, patting my hands, "you look beautiful. He's going to be stunned."

"That's the thing." I looked up at her. "The clothes I bought today were for me, not him."

"Aren't all the clothes for you and not him?"

I'd forgotten that yesterday I was wearing the dirty office clothes Vito likes.

"We always wear what we want, but it's alright to wear something you think the man you're interested in will like. There's no harm in that." She walked over to the counter and set her purse down. "Cortez, Tobias! Come in here!"

"Wait!" I whispered loudly as I rushed to her side at the counter. "I always thought it was wrong to dress for others?"

She smiled. "We've been told that, but it's not wrong, unless you're consumed by it. You have to be you, but there's nothing wrong with looking beautiful, or attractive. You never want to dress in something that's not your style, then you're being a fraud and making yourself miserable. But I don't see anything wrong with dressing nice for your," she paused, "*boss*." She blinked with wide eyes, and I almost drowned in embarrassment. Vito was my boss, and now I was here trying to make sure my boss still liked me. I felt like I'd fallen prey to some dirty cliché.

"Coming!" Vito called.

My heart almost leapt from my chest in a way it had never done before. Ever since Dafni told me that Vito loved me, and that I loved Vito, I couldn't help but feel nervous about seeing him.

"If you're that nervous," Dafni said as heavy footsteps came closer, "call him Cortez. It's his real name anyway."

The words hadn't registered when Vito rounded the corner. They'd been calling him Cortez this whole time, but it never clicked that Vito's name wasn't actually Vito. Cortez was the same name on his fake ID, which meant that ID wasn't fake at all.

"Wow," Vito's words were almost a whisper as he looked me over.

When I was left to pick out my own clothes, I didn't know what to buy. I was used to wearing sweatpants and oversized clothes at my old apartment. If I wasn't at work in slacks and a shirt, then I was in sweats and a t-shirt. I was always researching and studying so I wanted to be comfortable. Which put me at a loss when I needed to pick out my own clothes from luxury brands I hadn't even heard of. Fine silks, freshly pressed clothes, gold actually woven into the seams, I never imagined living a life like this. Thankfully, Dafni was there, and that's when the awkwardness from that conversation in the car began to melt.

She picked out things that would look good on me, but I didn't buy anything I didn't feel comfortable in. Turned out, I kind of liked the way I dressed as Vito's secretary. I just didn't want to look like a hooker.

Vito closed his hands into fists as he stared at me. Brown eyes traced my figure slowly in my simple pair of dark jeans, and a fitted orange sweater.

"You look," he swallowed, "really normal."

I blinked, unsure of what to say when his father reached up and smacked the back of Vito's head.

"Ow!" He whirled and looked up at his father. "Why'd you just hit me?"

"Because you said she looked normal and not incredible!"

"Dad!"

"Tobias!" Dafni said.

"Uh," I breathed, glancing around at everyone. I pushed past Vito and his father to race upstairs.

"Iyana, wait!" Vito called after me.

I slammed my door shut and leaned against it briefly. I felt so stupid, trying to be me when I didn't even know who "me" was. I rubbed my forehead and moved to the bed. Pulling out my duffle bag, I dug through it to put on something Vito was used to seeing me in. Tears pricked my eyes and my clothes started to blur as I dug furiously. Anything would do, but I just couldn't make myself stop caring so much. I didn't want to be ugly to him. I didn't want to be unattractive, but I didn't know if it was okay to feel so disappointed in myself. *When did I even begin to care what Vito thought of me?*

"What am I even doing?" I whispered.

"Iyana?" Vito knocked as he spoke.

"Go away," I called.

"Let me in."

"No."

"Please."

"No!"

He twisted the handle and came in anyway, but he stopped when he saw me sitting on the floor, a single tear running down my cheek.

"What?" I snapped.

He pushed the door closed and came and sat on the floor with me. "Iyana, what I said was stupid. I just didn't know what else to say."

"You said how you felt." I shrugged before setting my duffle bag on my lap.

"No, I didn't," he said. "It just didn't come out right."

I looked up at him, a pleading face stared back at me.

"I'm going to change." I stood, but Vito shot to his feet and tried to block me. I pushed past him, but before I could get to the door, he slammed a hand against it. I whirled around ready to snap, but we were so close—his hand against the door beside my head, leaning forward to say something. I bit my lip and looked away.

"I think you look like my secretary off duty, and I like it." He paused. "I like it a lot."

"Don't just say that because I'm upset."

"How can I prove to you that I'm not just saying this?"

I threw my hands up. "I don't know, Vito. I guess I'm just feeling really self-conscious."

"You shouldn't."

Brown eyes almost consumed me as he leaned closer, his lips grazing my cheek. He stopped by my ear, but no words came from him. Instead, he kissed my neck and placed his hand behind my back, pulling me against him. I silently appreciated his kisses, and when his hand began to slip down my back, I felt a stirring in my chest.

"Vito," I whispered.

"I don't want you to ever be self-conscious around me," he whispered against my neck.

I clenched my jaw, begging myself not to sound like I was weakened by his touch. "Ok," I muttered.

He pecked my neck again. "Good." When he stepped back and looked me over, he said, "You are an incredible woman, Iyana. All of you."

"Do you really mean that?"

"I do."

I sighed, covering my face as I felt the heat of embarrassment washing over it.

"Come on." He reached for my hand. "We've got to have lunch with my parents, and tonight I'm going to take you to dinner."

"Dinner? Like a date?"

"Yeah, a date."

I clutched his hand as we left my room. "Is it a fancy place?"

He looked up at the ceiling, bobbing his head for a second as he tried to come up with an answer. "It's not suit and tie fancy, but it's a nice place. I'm just not a suit and tie guy, so I had reservations made for somewhere less…"

"Suffocating?" I offered as we reached the bottom of the steps.

He nodded. "Exactly."

"Cortez, Iyana, lunch is ready," Dafni said as she stood in the archway of the dining room.

Vito nodded, leading me by the hand through their lovely home. When we came in to sit, I thought we'd be seated the way we were at dinner yesterday, however, the table had been altered. Vito's placement was at the opposite end of the table from his father. Dafni sat on Mr. Gerardo's right side, and my placement was on Vito's right side.

Vito noticed the change in seating as well, and he turned and whispered to me, "Seating has meaning in this family, and at BT, I just never enforce it. But my father's old-fashioned, and it looks like he's going to enforce it right now." I nodded and he continued, "If you take that seat by my side, that means that's your place, Iyana. It's like making a commitment."

Mr. Gerardo eyed me, and Dafni tilted her head and nodded at me. When I looked back at Vito, he looked worried.

"What's the problem?" I asked in a whisper.

"I don't want you to feel like you have to be committed to me or BT. You want to get out, but you can't get out until I do if you take that seat beside me."

His eyes were serious, and his words were forceful. But it didn't matter. For the past six months I'd sat at Vito's side, and I knew that I didn't know where else to sit now. It seemed like that was where I belonged.

"Vito, do you want me by your side?"

He studied me, quietly analyzing me the way he always did when I showed him mistakes on a spreadsheet. He never said much when he stared, but I could tell his mind was wandering somewhere I wanted to reach.

"Iyana, I don't want to influence your decision."

"Just answer the question."

He took a long pause.

"Yes, I want you by my side."

I nodded and went to stand behind my chair. Vito moved over to me and pulled it out for me as I sat down. Pushing me in, he moved to sit in his seat at the head of the table across from his father.

"Well," Mr. Gerardo said, "that is an important seat, Iyana. Are you sure you want to sit there?"

"I've sat in this seat every day for the last six months. It's mine to sit in."

Mr. Gerardo cracked a smile and nodded. "Very well, let's begin our lunch."

The waiters came out with large trays carrying salads and steaming soups.

"You two should get married," Mr. Gerardo said.

"Tobias!" Dafni snapped.

He raised a thick hand to her and looked between Vito and me. "She's been your right arm for six months, Cortez. Any woman who will stay longer than a month in this business is worth keeping, and you know that."

"Dad, we can talk about this later," Vito said without looking up.

"We can talk about it now," I said sternly.

The concern in Vito's eyes flared again and Mr. Gerardo gave me an approving nod. "He wants to protect you, and I told him the only way to protect you in this business is to stop treating you like you matter to him."

I raised a brow. "What do you mean?"

Mr. Gerardo raised his hand, signaling the waiter who was pouring mint water into his glass to stop.

"He means I have to make it seem like you don't matter to me," Vito explained.

"Wouldn't marrying me seal the deal, though?"

Vito shook his head. "In this life, you never marry for love, you marry for business and opportunity. The woman you actually love, you keep her locked away, as far removed from this world as possible."

It all clicked. Vito kept me locked in the tower and called me his princess because he loved me. But he doesn't want to marry me because he loves me.

My hands trembled and I tucked them into my lap, trying to hide the nerves swelling in my chest. I didn't want to be foolish and draw conclusions only to hurt myself. I let out a small breath, pushing away the thoughts of Vito loving me.

"In other words," Mr. Gerardo said, "if he marries you, it has to look like he married you for opportunity. You need to provide BT with something worth marrying for."

When Vito finally looked at me, I couldn't hold his gaze. I turned away, staring into the onion soup steaming in my bowl.

"Well," Mr. Gerardo cooed, "what can you offer BT?"

"I'm not marrying her," Vito said angrily.

"Vito, she's a good girl," Dafni said. "You should marry her. I'm sure she has plenty to offer you and the business."

"You don't understand, Mom," Vito shook his head.

"Well, I do," Mr. Gerardo chimed in, "and you need to marry her so—"

"I'm not marrying Iyana!"

"Why not!" Mr. Gerardo shouted.

"Because you loved Mom, and you couldn't protect her!" Vito breathed heavily, staring across the table at his parents. "I don't know if I can protect her. Dad, you did everything you could to keep Mom safe, and it still wasn't enough."

The silence was deafening and the Gerardos looked like they'd just heard the worst news in the world. I reached for Vito's hand, and when my hand touched his, he looked at me with an apology in his eyes.

"I'm a veterinarian." I turned and looked at Dafni and Tobias. "I can work with breeders to breed dogs that would be good for guarding. And I can train these dogs. But that's all I have to offer."

"It's a start," Mr. Gerardo said. "But we need something bigger."

Vito squeezed my hand as he said, "Iyana, you can't do this."

"It's only for a little while."

"Vito," Dafni called. Her voice was stern and motherly, and it caught Vito's attention. His tight jaw, and sunken eyes, Vito was stressed, but he'd never let me know it.

"You are a different man from your father. You can protect Iyana. You have to protect her. Or she'll end up doing something that puts both of you in danger in the hopes that you'll trust her. Don't shut her out."

I squeezed his hand. "We can do this."

"I've invested in gold," Vito said slowly.

Gerardo slowly crossed his arms, blinking as widely as his son. Vito looked at his mother. "Gold, diamonds, gems. I've invested in them all."

"And what good will that do?"

"Iyana will speak to the women in this world."

"As a housewife?" his dad asked flatly.

"No." Vito took a breath and looked at me. "If you want to win a war, you have to outsmart your enemy. Sometimes to outsmart them, you've got to do everything in a way they wouldn't expect."

"What do you mean?" I asked quietly.

"I mean, I'm going to marry you, Iyana, but I'm also giving my seat to you."

17

God is Gracious

I felt like I was losing myself, like I'd somehow forgotten my roots and my faith in the mix of everything. I'd whispered prayers casually, not even sure anymore if God was hearing me because I was in so deep.

Had I somehow let my feelings for Vito sway me into making a decision that would challenge my faith?

I claimed that I was only doing things because I had no choice, but every single time a choice fell into my lap, I ended up doing things that seemed to flat out oppose God. Staying with Vito when I didn't have to. Working for BT. Making sure this illegal business stayed afloat.

Where was God at in all of this? Why did I let my faith disappear?

"God, where are you?" I whispered as tears fell onto my

Bible.

Vito and I ended up returning home instead of going to dinner last night. We got into the Tower late, but I couldn't sleep much. I've been up, trying to figure out what I'm doing, and why God hasn't rescued me. Maybe I don't want to be rescued, or maybe I'm letting my feelings for Vito get in the way. *What do I do, God?* I sniffled as I opened my Bible.

Flipping through pages, reading over highlights, but a passage stopped me from turning the page. It was Romans the fifth chapter, and third verse.

And not only so, but we glory in tribulations also: knowing that the tribulation worketh patience; and patience, experience, and experience, hope: and hope maketh not ashamed; because the love of God is shed abroad in our hearts by the Holy Ghost which is given unto us.

I stared at the passage, wondering if this was from God, or if I was just trying to force it to be.

"It is from my Father."

I snapped my head up, and there was a Man, indescribable in beauty, an outpouring of light and kindness. I immediately recognized him.

"You are Jesus," I whispered.

"I am." He smiled. "I have been waiting for you here."

"Waiting for me?"

He stood from my bed and walked over to the desk. His white robe seemed to be made of light—not fabric at all. But I wasn't sure because He looked like light itself, the way it's supposed to look on Earth. Pure and raw luminescence, a glow bright enough to outshine the sun.

"Yes." He touched my hand and my mind felt at ease, like every stressful thought and tense muscle in my body was suddenly soothed. "I waited for you to come to this moment so that I could meet you here."

I stared at His hand on mine, the hole in his palm so fresh and red. I began to tremble.

"Why?" I whispered.

I couldn't break my gaze. He had really died for me, had really taken my pain away. There was proof right in front of me, yet, I was still angry, I was still hurt and confused. How could He have taken anything away if I still felt all the pain?

"You are broken inside."

I didn't know if He actually spoke or if His voice was just resonating within me.

"I am here to mend your brokenness."

"Why would You let me break if You loved me? Why didn't You just rescue me?"

His smile faded, and His eyes deepened with a great sadness. Tears began to blur His figure as I began to feel His pain. It was an aching love that was too heavy for me to bear. When I felt like I would crumble, His hand brushed my cheek, and suddenly the weight was lifted. I peered up at Him, but I didn't know what to say or to think. He was carrying around such sorrow, and it was all for me.

"It is not pleasing to God to see you broken, but it is in brokenness that often, My Father's children allow Him into their lives. Just like you, Iyana. You were seeking a solution to your situation. But I tell you the truth, I am your answer."

"How?" I murmured through tears, wishing so desperately that I could censor myself. But the words came freely, it was like because of His presence, I could only tell the truth. "How, when You haven't been here for me?"

"Are you angry at Me, or are you angry with yourself?"

I paused before I whispered, "I'm angry with myself. I shouldn't have stayed, and I made excuses for staying behind. Now I'm too far in, and I can't leave now. Vito needs me."

"You are right." He reached forward and brushed away my tears. "Cortez needs you."

I sniffled. "Then, has God given up on me because I decided to stay? Is Vito's need for me supposed to replace where God was in my heart?"

Jesus shook his head, dark hair swishing around Him with the movement. "No, My daughter, you are exactly where God needs and wants you to be. You are not too far from Him."

"How? How can He use someone like me who's turned their back on Him?"

"If you had truly turned away from God, you would not be here seeking Him out." He nodded at the open Bible on my desk. I turned to it, tracing the words I'd read.

"Do you remember what tribe My earthly bloodline came through?" Jesus came around the desk and peered over the Bible with me. He was tall and gentle and warm. When He stood beside me, there was a stirring in my heart, like I could weep for hours just because of His closeness.

"You mean like the Tribe of Judah?"

He nodded.

"Yes, I remember."

He reached forward and pulled my bookmark into my Bible. "We will come back to this. I want to show you something."

"Of course," I said. I watched Him turn the pages, wondering if this was really happening, or if I was making this up.

Jesus stopped turning the pages and said, "You are beginning to doubt My presence. I am here, Iyana." He turned and touched my cheek. "I am right here with you as I have always been."

"Then why can I see You when I never could before?"

"You needed to see Me in this state to keep believing."

I fell silent and my eyes drifted from His back to the Bible. It was open to the Book of Genesis, the thirty-eighth chapter.

"This is Judah and Tamar's story," I said, leaning closer.

He nodded. "Judah has relations with Tamar, and the result is pregnancy. Tamar bore Judah two sons, twins, Pharez and Zarah. Pharez is part of the earthly family of My bloodline."

"I don't understand why You're telling me this."

Jesus returned His gaze to the Word. "My Father allowed His children to see the mistakes of those whom people may hold to a higher standard. Many on earth believe that everyone in the Tribe of Judah lived purely or perfectly. But that is not so. Many have made decisions that are not in alignment with God. But God's plans are always fulfilled."

"What was His plan with Judah and Tamar?"

"The plan was not intended for Judah and Tamar to have children, but God needed a seed to bring the Son of Man into the Earth, and when Judah's sons were disobedient, the seeds birthed from Judah and Tamar were used by My Father."

I massaged my forehead, trying to make sure I understood it all. "So, you're saying that even though God had plans, me not leaving BT will somehow fulfill God's *original* plan?"

He smiled deeply. "You are correct. God's plan has always been to use Cortez to bring light to the darkness here in New York. He wants Cortez in His Kingdom. But he has fallen weak and lost his way."

I nodded.

"You brought the light back into his life, and if you had left BT, Cortez would have chased after your light."

I covered my mouth and tears began to fall again. "I ruined everything."

"No." Jesus grabbed my hands and pulled me up to my feet. "You have changed the course, but now the crown that was to be set upon Cortez's head will be set upon yours, and all of New York and those connected to Bellen Tupp will remember you."

"What?" I breathed deeply.

"Bellen Tupp is going to fall. It is the only way to save Cortez, and it is the only way to bring light to those wandering in the darkness of New York. Cortez and the citizens of this city will learn that God is gracious."

I stammered, trying to make sense of it all, trying to believe every word. But something about 'God is gracious' seemed familiar.

"God is gracious? Why did you say that?" He leaned forward and kissed my head. His scent was one I could not describe but I knew I would never forget it. I would never forget *any* of this, and I would search for His warmth forever— His kindness, His gentleness, His love in every person I met.

Stepping back, Jesus stood in the middle of my room, "My father calls to Me. You have been grafted into the beloved, and you will show God's grace to these people. That is why He named you 'Iyana.'"

Before I could speak, Jesus disappeared in a flash of light. I suddenly felt my own weight again and dropped to my knees. In His presence, I felt nothing but His kindness and goodness. It was the most beautiful thing I'd ever experienced.

I sat in a daze all morning as I put the pieces together of all that Christ had revealed to me. The plan of God was to stop gang violence and bring Cortez back to Him, but how could that happen with me sitting as the head of BT? I guess it didn't matter since that was the revised plan.

I wanted to hate myself for not leaving when I'd had the chance, especially after I found out I was no longer considered missing. But my disappointment was pointless. Jesus Christ Himself just told me I can and will still be used by God.

I took a deep breath and forced myself to smile as I climbed into bed. I wouldn't let myself worry or doubt God anymore, but I wanted to start making better decisions. Now that I knew the plans of God, I wanted to do my part.

I laid down and pulled the blankets over my head as the tingling feeling of joy crept over me. A loud knock came from the door, waking me up out of my sleep. I glanced around for my clock, and found it was after ten in the morning. Throwing the blankets back, I raced to my front door, already knowing Logan was there because Hardy was still sulking and Vito was too worried.

I snatched my door open, ready to apologize, but was lost for words as I found Vito standing there, holding a bouquet of flowers.

"Hi," he said stiffly.

"Hi," I said back.

"I know I promised we'd go to dinner last night, but we really needed to get home."

I sighed, thinking of how we'd rushed back to the Tower—jetting off in Vito's private plane to fly across the country in the middle of the night.

"I wanted to apologize," Vito said.

I chuckled as I reached for the flowers. "I overslept. I wasn't feeling very well this morning, and when I started feeling better, I fell asleep."

He exhaled heavily. "Oh, I thought you were mad at me."

I giggled as I inhaled the pink and red flowers. "These are beautiful, thank you."

He nodded. "Can I come in for a second?"

"Of course." I stepped back, allowing Vito inside.

As I set the flowers on the counter, I watched him looking

around at the apartment. His dark hair was tucked under a baseball cap, and he was wearing a hoodie that was baggy on him.

"We need to tell everyone the plans."

"The plans?" I murmured as I cut the stems on my flowers.

"Our wedding."

I snipped my finger, splitting it open so a red sea could pour from it.

"Iyana," he said as I whined in pain. He grabbed my hand and ran it under cold water. We silently watched the blood rinse down the drain, both of us trying to think of something to say. It wasn't that I wanted to keep the marriage a secret, it was something I felt nervous about, especially knowing that BT would fall by my hands. Prolonging the wedding would be in my best interest, however, prolonging it may not be what God wants.

Vito stopped the water and folded a paper towel for me to hold against my finger.

"The med kit is in my bathroom."

He nodded and went to retrieve it. I stood in the kitchen, staring at my bleeding finger. Thoughts of the fresh wounds I saw on Jesus's hands took my breath away, and I was doubled over with tears when Vito came inside.

"Does it hurt that bad?" he asked as he set the medical kit on the table.

"What if I told you BT was going to fall apart?"

He froze. I could see his figure through my tears but not his face. I hunched over, staring at the floor when Vito dropped his arms.

"When I was a child," he started, "I had a dream that I was a king. My kingdom was large and vast, and instead of living in a castle, I lived in a single tower." He took a breath. "And one day, while sitting on my throne, a slender figure in all white came into the throne room. A chair—a throne—more elegant and beautiful than mine was raised from the ground beside me. Then the faceless, nameless woman came and sat on it."

He paused, shoving his hands into his pockets. "I looked over at her, completely enamored by her beauty. Even though I had no idea who she was, I wanted to give her everything if it meant she would stay with me. So I took my crown off and placed it on her head. And in that moment, the Tower began to fall apart around us. And then I woke up."

I didn't want to lift my head to see his face, but he squatted in front of me, and forced me to make eye contact with him. He was holding a weak smile, and lazy eyes I could barely see beneath his cap.

"I couldn't forget that dream, and I couldn't forget the way I felt when I woke up. I've searched for that feeling and when I saw you, it returned. It's hard to describe what exactly I felt, besides happiness, but I knew you would take my place and make BT fall when this feeling resurfaced after taking you in."

"But why?" I asked quietly. "Why go through all of this? Marry me and sit me there, when you knew BT would fall apart?"

He leaned forward and grabbed my hands. "Because the most memorable part of the dream was that when the woman first sat on the throne, she wasn't smiling. But when I crowned her, and the Tower began to crumble, she finally smiled. And even though I'd lost everything, seeing her smile was worth losing it all."

"A smile? A smile was worth losing it all? Vito that—"

"It wasn't just a smile," he said absently, "it was the reason she was smiling. Freedom. Being free made her happy."

"And all I wanted when I arrived was freedom."

Silence teased us as I finally stood upright. Vito slowly rose to his feet, never taking his eyes off me.

"You're really okay with this?" I asked.

"I don't have a choice."

"I'm sorry," I whispered dryly.

"We should probably get your finger cleaned," he said, casually changing the subject. "You might bleed through that napkin."

I hadn't realized I'd still been bleeding until Vito said something. I wanted to press the issue further, but I knew it was better this way. It was clear Vito had dealt with his feelings about BT falling, and I didn't want to make him relive those feelings.

Opening the kit, he pulled out alcohol and a bandage.

"Is that alcohol?" I said nervously.

He looked at the bottle in his hand, and then at me. "Speaking of alcohol, do you want a dry wedding?"

I looked off for a second, and said timidly, "I hadn't thought about it."

"It's only been a day," he said. "But I do want to have it as soon as possible after the New Year."

Before I could answer, there was a burning in my finger, and I almost shed a tear. I snatched my finger from Vito to stare at it. "What did you do?"

He looked up, a smile on his lips, his eyes barely visible beneath the visor of his cap. "I cleaned it."

"I absolutely hate you."

The awkwardness in the air finally shifted and we both let out a small laugh as the burning began to settle. I watched him slowly opening a bandage, and I wondered about him. How much Vito really knew about BT, how much he chose to let go. Who was he really, who was Vito or Cortez?

I cleared my throat in the quiet between us as he wrapped the bandage around my finger.

"Hey, Vito? Who is Cortez Ortega?"

He stopped and glanced up at me. "Why?"

"Your parents never called you 'Vito,' not even once."

He began wrapping my finger again before cutting the bandage. "My real name is Cortez Ortega. Vito Gerardo is the name I took on to carry on the Gerardo legacy."

"But isn't your father's last name Gerardo? Why is your real last name Ortega?"

He studied me for a second before he grunted, "Seems like you already know the answer."

My words were caught in my throat, and I couldn't speak.

"They don't know that I know I'm not a Gerardo—that my mother's maiden name is the one they gave me to protect me if I ever got out of BT. When I was a child, my family told me I couldn't be a Gerardo until I was older. It was just a fake name I believed Tobias went by. But, taking the seat as leader of the Pack, you learn a lot about the past."

"I see," I said as he packed up the medical kit.

"Were you going to tell me that you knew I wasn't a Gerardo?"

His eyes searched mine, but I didn't know what answer he was looking for, and I didn't want to lie, either.

"I was waiting for the war to be over. I didn't think it was something you needed to know during a time like this."

He nodded. "Fair enough."

--- BT ---

Vito gathered Logan, Hardy, Kat, and Leo into his loft to make the announcement. Kat and Leo were requested since they would be in charge of the guest list, security, the venue, and preparing for the wedding. Vito put them in charge so they could make sure nothing suspicious happened with the plans or get leaked before time—and also because I liked Kat.

"Boss?" Kat called as Vito stepped out of his office. He needed to check something before making our wedding announcement, but Kat interrupted before he could even speak.

"Yeah?" Vito said as he came over.

"I spoke with Rion earlier; he was picking up some packages for me when he spotted this." She passed him a postcard.

"It's a black-tie event," Vito said as he read it. "Why is this important?"

"Because of the name of one of the speakers."

Vito's brows lowered and he looked over the postcard once more. "Timothy Walters."

My ears burned as everyone looked over at me.

"He's running for mayor," Kat added. Her eyes frowned as she mouthed an apology to me.

My father was running for mayor, but I had no real understanding of his actions.

"I'll take care of it," Vito said as he passed her back the card.

Logan folded his arms and said, "If he's in office and not one of our guys, then that'll be a problem, boss."

I glanced over at Hardy who hadn't spoken, but his tense demeanor was a louder response.

"I know, but it'll be fine."

"How are you not worried? Everything we've worked for can fall apart," Logan pleaded.

"I said it'll be fine because I'm starting a new business that people are going to want to invest in." He reached for me, and I took his hand. "Also, Iyana and I are getting married. She's going to be head of the Woof Pack."

"You're kidding, right? Iyana as leader of the Pack?" Logan's eyes darted to mine. "I'm not opposed to the marriage, or even her taking over—but only if she can actually do the job."

"Well, it's not up to you, Logan," Vito said, looking around the small group. "This is the best way to protect Iyana and win this war. You want BT to still stand when this war is over? Then we need Iyana at the top."

It took everything in me not to whirl around and yell at Vito that BT would not be standing for long. But he avoided eye contact with me, and it was all I needed. Destroying the hope of those who worked for him was far more damaging than letting the events play out on their own.

"Fine," Leo said, stepping forward. He had icy blonde hair and light brown skin, appearing more like a prince and less like a guard dog. "We know Iyana's good for it." He nodded at me. "But what about the clients? What will they think?"

"That's why we needed a business plan, to bring in new clients and threaten our old ones with being replaced, while also giving them the first bite at an investment."

"You should go to this event, then," Kat said. "Make a big announcement there that Iyana's taking over and you're getting married. People will automatically think that the marriage is for some kind of exchange if you're going public with someone they don't know about. People will want to invest on the spot."

"I agree," I said nervously. "Announcing our marriage will draw people in, but announcing me as the next leader of BT, despite your reputation, will cause people to want to know more."

"But how much more? What if they think you can't do it?" Logan shrugged. "BT's never had a woman as the leader."

"Technically," I said, "it'll be a partnership. Vito will have forty-five percent ownership of BT, and I'll have fifty-five. But his opinion and voice will be needed, so his clients will have some security that I'm not fully taking over without Vito."

"I think this is a good plan," Hardy spoke up for the first time. "But think about the women in this business. They're going to start wanting more say."

"Then let's give it to them." I stepped into the center of the room. "Let's stop treating the women as prizes and treat them like the winners *of* the prize. We do that, we create more clients."

Kat nodded in approval, a smile slowly creeping onto her face. "You'll double the clientele with men *and* women now searching for products, and you'll pull some places apart. At that point, BT can absorb those smaller places in need of cash."

We all looked around at each other, wondering if this was actually going to work, while Vito and I knew it wouldn't.

"A plan this large and widespread will take time. But it'll give us leverage in this war. So if smaller clients or even larger clients are taken by Grizzly, we'll be covered," Vito explained.

"When's the event?" I asked.

"Next week," Kat answered.

"Then we have a week to start making preparations to have something tangible for that event."

18

Mrs. Jefferson Doesn't Know a Thing

I was lying in bed, flicking through the channels, when my wife came in and closed the bedroom door. "Junior did not want to go to bed tonight. He was excited," she said, "since this was the first time you were home all night in a while."

"That's a lie." I looked at her briefly before returning my eyes to the television. "I was just home all night last week. And I came to his game, didn't I? He's going to have to toughen up a little. Maybe you should stop babying him."

She scoffed and I caught her out the corner of my eye placing her hands on her hips. "Excuse me? Brandon, I wouldn't have to baby him if his father was ever home. I don't even know what to tell him about your work! I have nothing to say when he asks what you do all day or why you're going out of town *again* because I don't even know what you really do at your firm! You're so secretive, and it worries me."

I sighed loudly and tossed the remote onto the bed. I threw the covers off my legs as I got out the bed to head to the living room.

"Where are you going? We're talking, Brandon."

I kept walking. I was not in the mood to hear her bickering at me for not telling her everything. When I married her, I told her I couldn't tell her much about the firm I was working for because they were a private practice. She was fine with it then. Now it's a big deal. I shook my head as I tried not to let the thoughts annoy me and make me do something I'd regret like I've done in the past.

"Are you seriously not going to answer me, Brandon!?"

"Alex!" I snapped around to face her. Her big eyes were filled with tears, a hand on her bulging belly and she huffed loudly like walking behind me had taken all of her energy.

"I'm tired of feeling like I'm on the outside of your life," she complained. "I am your *wife*... if no one else knows everything about you, *I* should. But I know nothing, and that is not right." She turned away and headed back to the bedroom.

"Alex," I called.

She stopped, looking over her shoulder with pouty lips.

"I have a black-tie event tomorrow night. I want you to come with me and meet some of my coworkers."

Her eyes widened and she turned to face me fully. "You're not serious?"

I nodded as I came down the hall to her. The engagement

was mostly for me to make connections while Tim gave a speech. There wouldn't be anyone around who would want to blow my cover, especially since Grizzly wouldn't be there. And it would keep Alex off my back for a while which was what I needed right now. I'll just lose her in the crowd to mingle and find her after I've done some business.

"I am serious." I placed my hands on her waist. "Keeping my work life separate from my home life is causing too many problems between us and I don't like it. I want you to trust me, to know that your husband is out doing all he can to make this lifestyle possible for you."

She nodded as she draped her arms over my shoulders. "Oh, my goodness. Brandon, this is all I've wanted for so long. Thank you." She hopped to her tiptoes and kissed me.

--- BT ---

As we rode in the car together, Alex fiddled with her hands. They had swelled up over the last seven months, but today was a good day for her, they didn't look as fat as usual. I reached over and interlaced my fingers with hers to stop the fiddling. Raising her hand to my lips, I kissed it to calm her down.

"You look beautiful, Lex."

She took a deep breath and wiped a hand over her smoothed curls that were pulled into a complicated bun. "Brandon, you're just making me more nervous," she teased. "We haven't been out together in such a long time, and I've never met any of your colleagues. Now they have to meet your fat pregnant wife."

I snorted as I turned into the parking lot of the event hall. "Alex, you can't help that you're bigger right now. I mean that's a seven-month-old child in there, you're going to be pretty big."

"I couldn't even wear heels tonight," she complained as she took her seatbelt off.

"Hey," I leaned over and kissed her, "everyone's going to love you."

Her brows fell into a saddened look. "And what if they don't?"

"Then you'll understand why I hate work and never talk about it."

She cracked a smile and began to laugh.

I leaned back to unbuckle my seatbelt. "And you'll still have me. I'll always love you Alex, no matter what."

She blushed deeply.

"Come on," I said, getting out the car, "let's get inside. I want you to meet a few people."

It was a dangerous thing to do, bringing my wife—my *real* wife—to this event, however, this event wasn't filled with gangbangers and candy shop owners. There would be city officials here, upstanding citizens interested in the good of the city. Having a pregnant woman on your arm made it look like your intentions were pure.

As long as I wasn't too snuggly with her, I was certain my business partners and potential partners would think it was all for show. Alex would fit in just fine.

As we stepped inside, the place was crawling with possibilities. I couldn't be a gang member tonight, I had to be a loving husband supporting his best friend's campaign. It was hard not to be a gang member, because that's all I've been for most of my life. Rarely, do I have to be sophisticated or even interact with people who weren't part of a gang or interested in what we had to offer.

I took a deep breath and forced the smile I'd learned to hold that looked genuine and *not* forced. I darted my eyes around to find Tim, and I spotted him standing by a table, reading his notecards. A feeling of relief washed over me, and I was thankful that for once he wouldn't stiff me.

"Come on, Alex, there's someone I'd like to introduce you to," I said, pulling her along.

I had to be picky with who she talked to. Had to make sure she wouldn't talk to someone she would see in a grocery store or while she was out picking up BJ. I had to introduce her to people I could trust, and people who owed me something.

"Tim," I called as I walked up to his table. His eyes were just as emotional as Iyana's. I tried not to imagine her as Tim looked up at me. His gaze immediately fell on Alex, snaking over her like a serpent on a vine.

"Brandon," he said, finally returning his eyes to mine. "How are you?" He tried to sound chirpy as he extended a hand to me.

I took it and nodded. "Never better, Tim. I'd like to introduce you to my wife, Alex."

Tim nodded slowly before extending a hand to her. "It's a

pleasure to meet you."

Alex smiled gullibly and took his hand. "The pleasure is all mine, really. You work with Brandon at the firm?"

He almost reacted in a manner of uncertainty, but he caught himself at the last second. Never bothering to glance my way, Tim chuckled, "No, I'm actually an old friend of Brandon's. I used to work at the firm, but my wife fell ill, so I retired."

"Oh, I'm so sorry. Is she any better?"

The words hung heavily in the air between us, but Tim only took a breath and shrugged.

"Doctors don't know what's wrong now. Illness seems to be gone, but for some reason," he finally looked over at me, subliminally villainizing me, "she just won't wake up. Isn't that right, Brandon?"

"You've been to see her?" Alex asked, looking up at me.

I patted her hand wrapped around my arm and gave Tim a long stare before looking down at Alex. "Yes, on one or two occasions. I was assigned to bring her flowers."

"How lovely." She looked back at Tim. "I would love to send her flowers and stop by to see her sometime. I'm sure she'd like some company."

"Oh no, Mrs. Jefferson, I wouldn't want to put you out of your way."

She waved a hand. "It's no bother at all. I'm learning how to crotchet, so I've been making our little one some new shoes. The time I spend alone at home while Brandon's at work and Junior's at school, I can be there. I'd honestly love to come."

Tim flinched when she mentioned Junior. No one knew about him, and I didn't need that spreading around and some kind of way getting back to Jewels.

"Alright," I interrupted, "I'll get Alex the information for the hospital. We're going to mingle elsewhere so you can prep for your speech."

"You're speaking tonight?" Alex asked excitedly.

Tim nodded.

"I can't wait to hear it," she beamed.

"I appreciate your support, Mrs. Jefferson."

She nodded, and I tugged on her as we stepped away. I looked back, eyeing Tim harshly, but he blinked away, back to his cards.

"That man was very kind. His poor wife, I wonder if he has any kids—"

"Alex," I interrupted as we weaved through the crowd.

"Yes?"

I could hear the confusion in her voice, and I tried to explain kindly, "It's not good to always talk about kids and family life. These people are political, they want to hear politics."

"I see. Did that maybe stir him before he speaks tonight?"

"Yeah." I nodded.

"I see. I'll try to keep it political, then. I don't want to mess anything up for you and your friends."

I stopped and leaned down to peck her cheek. "Thank you, Lex."

She reattached herself to my arm and we swayed through

the crowd. This was one of the first events Alex and I had ever been to. We used to go on dates, and she'd link on to me the way she was now, and I felt like there was no place I'd rather be than beside her. But work became overbearing, and when I considered getting out, I couldn't. I needed to stay in, and she became a liability. I started treating her like one too, but as we moved through the crowd, my heart stirred in a way that it hadn't in a long time. She was the only person in the world who could make me feel this way, and for a second, I thought my heart had returned. But then I spotted Jewels, and my heart deflated, but there was a stirring somewhere else in my body—one that responded directly to lust.

"Alex," I leaned over so she could hear me. "I'm going to the restroom. I need you to wait here at the bar for me."

She sighed. "You're not going to leave me here forever, right? Going off and mingling while I'm pregnant and sucking down all the water?"

I chuckled. "I won't be away for long." I kissed the top of her head and tossed a wad of cash on the counter. "Get her anything she wants except for alcohol," I said to the bartender. He nodded, and I took my leave to maneuver through the crowd.

I searched for her, moving slowly through the finely dressed people. Every red piece of fabric caught my attention, and I hoped it was Jewels. Moving deeper into the crowd, I found her standing by a pillar, talking to a man. I lingered close enough so she could see me, but far enough away so no one else knew I was watching her. She seemed to be enjoying this man, and when she coyly turned away, she caught my gaze. Her eyes widened, and she returned back to the man she was entertaining.

"Brandon? Fancy this!" A heavy hand clamped down on my shoulder, and I turned to face its owner. It was Xavier Hemmindale, a cousin to the Stolls family. He was a tall slender man, dark hair in a black suit with his signature golden pocket watch chain glinting out of his breast pocket.

"X." I reached for his hand. "How are you? How's that school going again? Something about accelerated learners, right?"

He nodded after taking a sip from his glass. "Yes, it's going very well. We just took in a young lady who is highly intelligent. She's going to be the face of this program, I can tell already."

I nodded, casually glancing over my shoulder. Jewels was still there talking and laughing, and I looked back at Hemmindale. "And the Stolls? How are they?"

He shrugged. "If you're asking if they want to keep doing business, then I'll say good. But if you're thinking they're still considering making those payments just to you, then not so good." He waved his hand around. "They're on the fence because Vito was pretty impressive in that meeting. They'd never met the guy, but Mrs. Stoll seems to love him."

"He's poisoned them," I hissed. "I never should've brought him along."

He took another sip of his drink. "Well, unfortunately, that's true. After all these years, they're actually considering making a direct payment to BT next month."

I grinded my teeth so hard I thought I'd flattened them when I opened my mouth to speak again, "Is there anything you can do? You know I'm good for it. And I need this deal, X."

He studied me, and then he sighed. "I'll give them a call in the morning and see what I can do. But no promises."

I clapped my hands together and thanked him. "I appreciate it so much. This really means a lot."

"I know you're a hard worker. Going against the Apple's Prince can be hard."

"Why are you helping me?"

"Because that's what old friends do. We pull strings for each other and try to influence where we can for old time's sake."

"I think I just felt something." I teasingly patted my chest.

Xavier leaned back and cackled loudly, and I took a glance over my shoulder again, but Jewels was gone. I turned back to Xavier and said, "Would you excuse me a minute?"

"Of course." He held up his glass. "I've got to find another one of these."

I brisked through the crowd looking for her when she stepped out a few paces ahead. She looked me over, calling red lips and a daring red dress with a split up the front so high I began to salivate. I watched her round hips sway as she walked through the crowd, and I followed her slowly. The sweeping red gown had a satin trail that followed behind her, catching everyone's attention. A few loose curls hung down to tickle her bare shoulders, and I almost couldn't wait any longer to see her. She rounded the corner, and I waited a moment before following. When I came around the corner, she snatched me into her embrace and forced her lips over mine.

"Where have you been?" she whispered between kisses.

"Does it matter? I'm here," I said.

She gasped into my mouth, begging me for more, whispering how much she missed this. "I didn't know you'd be here."

I ran my hand up her thigh, slipping beneath the material of her dress. Then I frowned. "You didn't wear underwear."

"Girl's gotta eat," she said slyly.

I pulled away. "What do you mean?"

She stepped back and folded her arms. "They found out you were the rat, and now I'm out of a job. I'm on a twenty-four-seven lockdown when I'm at the Tower."

"So, just leave. Come to the warehouse, I'll take you to my place."

That was a lie because I didn't have any other place but my house with Alex.

She shook her head. "You don't get it; they're always on me. I barely got away to see you tonight."

"See me tonight?" I paused. "Wait a second, who are you here with?"

Her nostrils flared and turned bright red, and my heart almost stopped.

"You brought them here to spy on me, didn't you?"

"I had no idea you were even here, Brandon. You know I would never do that!" She reached for my hand, but I took a step back.

"Don't ever speak to me again," I said.

"Brandon, wait! You can't do this!"

She rushed after me, but I whirled around and pinned her against the wall. Tears rolled down her cheeks as she said, "I would never betray you. They don't know you're here, either. That means you still have the upper hand."

I looked her over, and there was a twinge of pain in my chest for her. Jewels had never betrayed me, and had done everything I'd ever asked of her, even spending all Saturday with Grizzly for me.

"Please," she whispered, "you have to believe me."

Her red lips begged me to kiss them, and I did. Forcing my mouth over hers, I let her arms go, and she worked quickly to loosen my belt.

19

The Prince of the City

As our car pulled up to the hall, I stepped out and came around the side to open the door for Iyana. She stepped out in a floor-length black gown that hugged her body in the right places. Her hair was pulled up to the very top of her head, elongating her neck and showing off her beauty. She was breathtaking as she walked in black pumps with red leather on the bottom.

"You look stunning," I said, taking her hand.

Her shy eyes smiled at me as she said, "As do you, Vito. I've never seen you dressed up before."

I shrugged, closing the car door. "I hate it, honestly."

She chuckled as she clutched my arm, and we walked the steps into the hall. All eyes were on Iyana as we stepped in. I'd never told her what they called me around here because I hated it. I was no prince, and I didn't do anything good that a prince would do for his people. I sold drugs and did dirty business. Why all of New York thought that was something to uphold was beyond me.

"It's the Apple's Prince," a woman gawked as Iyana and I stepped by her.

"The Apple's Prince?" Iyana whispered.

I nodded at a few friends. "They call me the Prince of the City. I don't know why, though."

Iyana nodded at a few onlookers as we stopped at a table with a familiar face.

"Gio, Emilia," I said happily.

Emilia's face lit up when she saw us and ran to hug us. Her perfume smelled of grapes and sugar, and she wore a sequined dress in her favorite color—purple. Gio came over and shook my hand after Emilia finally let me go, sporting a matching purple suit.

"I haven't seen you two in ages! How's everything going?" Emilia asked as she went back to her table.

"Things are good." I smiled.

She eyed Iyana for a moment. "Vito, what's different about her? She doesn't look like a scared secretary anymore."

Gio chuckled. "She looks like a happy wife."

"*Fiancé*," Iyana corrected.

Gio's and Emilia's smiles flattened for a moment before their cheery smiles returned and they burst into celebration.

"Oh my goodness! Congratulations!" Emilia squealed as she hugged us again.

Gio grunted with a cheer as he shook my hand firmly and

slapped my shoulder. "I cannot believe this. I told you, she's a keeper."

"You were right about that," I said.

Iyana blushed as she grabbed onto me nervously.

"Let's get drinks!" Emilia exclaimed, but I waved her off.

"Sorry guys, we've got to make our way through the crowd. But keep our engagement a secret until the end. We're planning on making an announcement tonight."

Emilia nodded and slipped a gloved finger to her lips. "We won't tell a soul."

"Thank you."

I placed a hand on Iyana's back and guided her through the crowd. We walked quietly for a moment before she nervously said, "I thought it was alright to tell them."

"That was a good call, I was planning to tell them anyway."

She smiled, but it was a distracted one. She was watching every face in the crowd, looking for her father.

"I'm looking for him too, and so is Hardy and Logan and Kat."

"I know. I guess I just want to find him before he finds me. I don't even know what I'd say. I'll probably just avoid him."

"You don't have to be afraid of him," I said as I spotted the next client I wanted to speak with.

"I'm not scared," Iyana said flatly. "I just don't know what to say."

"Well, we'll have to cross that bridge when we get to it. I need your head focused for this next client."

"Who is he?" She looked around.

"There's a man in a crimson suit up ahead. We won't mention our engagement, just small talk. Jewels will find her way to him during the after-party to secure our business with him."

"Is that why you brought her along? To charm our clients?"

"Only the weak ones," I said as we got closer.

"Mr. Springstun, what a pleasure," I said with an extended hand.

"The Prince of the City, the pleasure is always mine." He took my hand and shook it firmly.

"Springstun, this is Iyana. Iyana, this is Mr. Springstun. He's a long-time friend of mine—one of the first clients I worked with when I took over the agency."

Iyana stepped forward and offered her hand. Springstun took it and kissed it. The flattery on her face almost made me punch Springstun, but instead, I gave him a stiff smile.

"Any friend of Vito's, is a friend of mine."

Mr. Springstun smiled wolfishly. "So I guess that makes us friends, doesn't it?"

"Absolutely," Iyana said sensuously. And then it hit me, Iyana was better at this than I thought. Her edgy voice and gentle smile were making Springstun melt in her hands.

He licked his lips as he stepped a little closer to Iyana. "You like Princes, I take it?"

"I like fishing," she said. "Making a big catch is only part of the enjoyment." Her wit almost knocked me off my feet. I didn't think Iyana had it in her, but she wasn't afraid like I thought she'd be.

"I see." Mr. Springstun grinned. "Do you ever enjoy the fish?"

"I've got tanks of them. Some just to marvel at … and others," she took a step and closed the gap between the two of them, "I plan to eat and enjoy."

His brow quirked. "Sounds like my type of woman."

"You have no idea," Iyana teased. She stepped back and grabbed my arm. "We'll be seeing you, Mr. Springstun."

He chewed his lip, and I offered him a nod as we turned and left him there. I pulled Iyana off to the first empty table I could find.

"What was that?"

Her chest was heaving quickly, and I realized she was nervous. She hadn't breathed at all while she stood there with Mr. Springstun.

"I was just trying to help," she explained. "I want people to know that I'm just as strong as you are. If they think I'm weak they may not want to do business with us."

I sighed and leaned over to kiss her head. "Just don't overdo it."

She nodded.

I sighed again. "I'm going to step over here for a second, I want you to mingle on your own. Don't tell anyone you know me, just introduce yourself, alright? It'll help people get familiar with you so that when we make the announcement, they won't feel so blindsided."

"Alright," she said as she regained herself.

"You did well back there."

She smiled up at me but didn't say anything else before walking off in the opposite direction. I watched as she moved to mingle with the single men; now it was my turn to mingle with whomever I could before the event started.

"Vito." Jewels came up to me out of the crowd and pulled me aside.

"What?" I snapped.

"I just saw Brandon while I was talking with a man named Abraham Abdul. I lost him in the crowd, but I know he'll come looking for me."

"What? Why is he here?"

She shrugged. "I don't know, but I'll go find out."

"Good, then find me or Iyana, got it?"

She nodded and stepped past me into the wandering crowd while I made my way back through the sea of people and found Kat and Rion chatting amongst themselves. Kat looked oddly nice in her gold pants-suit and her hair loose down her back. I'd only seen her a number of times with her hair down, and that was years ago. She actually looked like a kind young woman with it down, versus how strong and intimidating she could look with it up.

"Kat, Rion, what are you two doing? Rion, didn't I tell you to watch Jewels? That's the only reason you're here. Not to flirt with the head of my security."

He set his drink down on the table and nodded. "Yes, sir. I'll go find her."

"Thank you," I said curtly. I waited until he was out of sight to tell Kat, "Brandon's here."

"What?"

"Yeah, and Jewels spotted him."

"Well, do you think they're working together?"

"I don't know yet. But I need you keeping your eyes peeled for him. I need to know what he knows, and who he's here with and who he's backing."

She pulled out her phone. "I'm letting Leo know to keep an eye out for him, and to let me know if he sees him."

"Good, we can't let him out of our sights. Have you seen Iyana's father?"

She closed her phone and shook her head. "I haven't seen him at all. I talked to Logan a few minutes before I found Rion just wandering around; he said he hadn't seen him either."

I nodded. "Anyone checked in with Hardy?"

"Last time I saw him, I think he was getting a client."

I snorted. "Are you serious?"

She laughed. "He actually seemed to be really into it. We'll just have to wait and see."

"Alright." I nodded. "I'm going to make a few more friends before I take Iyana backstage. You remember where everyone is supposed to sit right?" I'd given her specific instructions on where everyone should sit or stand to watch the entire room. That way, they could tell me who was buying whose speech, and what the reactions were to the wedding announcement.

"Of course." She nodded.

20

Spin

I walked through the crowd, looking for people who looked approachable while still hunting for my father. I wanted to find him mostly for the sake of BT, but also because I needed to see him for myself. I needed to know why he was hurting mom, and why he stopped looking for me. My father has always plagued my mind, but it's different now than when I first arrived at BT. I used to wonder if he was alright or too worried about me being taken. Now, I'm trying to figure out what exactly my father is doing, what he has going on.

"Tim Walters! The man of the hour," a voice rang out behind me, and I turned to find a tall, thick man shaking hands with my father. I was frozen in place, unsure what to say or do, but my feet took the liberty of making a decision and brought me right up to his table.

"Mr. Walters," I said.

The thick tall man turned to see me, and he exclaimed, "I'm sorry, I didn't see you there."

I nodded at him, but my father didn't move. He stood stiffly, his hands glued to the table and his eyes locked on mine.

"Do you two know each other?" the tall man asked.

"Not very well," I said curtly, before turning to the man. "Can you give us a minute?"

He nodded, passing looks between us. "We'll talk soon, Tim."

"Iyana, what are you doing here?" my father asked me once the man had left.

"Why did you stop looking for me?"

"How do you know about that?"

"Just answer the question."

He gathered his cards in his hands, tapped them on the table a moment before answering, "Iyana, things are complicated right now. I had to do it."

"Why? And what are you doing to Mom?"

He squinted, and a scowl took over his features. "You think I'm hurting your mother?"

"I don't know anymore, Dad. I don't know what's going on or why you're doing any of the things you're doing. Like running for mayor. You've never liked politics."

"Things changed," he said flatly.

"I can see that."

"You have no idea what I've been through, so don't come over here acting like you're high and mighty when you aren't.

I know you're wrapped up in some gang."

"You know nothing," I snapped.

He shook his head, glancing around at the people walking by. I offered a few nods and smiles as people passed, trying not to make a scene with my father. He was standing right before me, and all I felt was anger. I didn't care how bad off he was or how much he'd been through. I needed answers, I needed to know what was actually going on with him and who put him up to running for mayor—if anyone at all.

"Dad, I need to know who put you up to this."

He shook his head again. "Don't ever ask me about my situation when I know nothing about yours."

"As if you ever gave me a chance to tell you," I said hotly. "You thought I was gallivanting around with a gang and closed the door in my face. Forced me to stay with those very same people you locked me out for being with."

Tears swelled in his eyes, and he hung his head. "Iyana, I can't tell you because it'll get me, and your mother killed."

I stammered for a moment, forcing myself not to pity him. "So, I guess you're only concerned for Mom then, which is crazy because you're the one keeping her in that hospital."

He slammed a hand on the table, drawing some eyes. I waved them off, patting the table myself and pretended to laugh heartily.

"I'm sorry, Iyana, alright? Is that what you want to hear?"

"I want the truth," I said, "but I guess I won't get that." I clutched my purse and turned to leave, rushing through the crowd for the bathroom when I spotted Brandon. He gripped his belt, and then pulled his zipper closed. I whirled around and moved away from him, trying to figure out why he was here, and what he had been doing around the corner from the bathrooms that he couldn't do *in* the bathrooms.

I rushed blindly to the bar and leaned against it, trying to calm myself down.

"Are you alright?"

I glanced up to find a woman. She was very pregnant, but she had a kind voice. She shuffled over to me and placed a hand on my back. "You came over in such a rush, I thought you were going to faint."

"I'm sorry," I said, standing upright. "I needed to get away from the crowds."

"I assume you're not a social butterfly?" She took her place back on the stool where her small clutch sat.

"No, I'm really an introvert, so this is a lot for me."

"I'm very social. I love talking, although, my husband seems to no longer be as social as I am." Her smile flinched and she turned away, looking at the cola in her glass.

"I'm sorry," I said.

She looked over at me and shrugged. "It can't be helped. You married?"

"Not yet." I smiled warmly at the thought of Vito.

"Look at you. Just the thought of him makes you shine like a star. You are absolutely stunning, Ms. ...?"

"Iyana Walters," I said, "soon to be Gerardo."

"Gerardo? I think I've heard that name before." She squeezed her straw between her two fingers and thought for a moment. "I believe my husband's old boss was Gerardo. I don't know." She shook her head. "He's had two boss changes in the last six years. I don't know what kind of firm this is, but it's crazy to me."

I stared blankly at her side profile as she sipped from her straw. "I'm sorry, I didn't catch your name."

"Oh dear! My name's Alex Jefferson. I'm here with my husband, Brandon Jefferson."

I fought the urge to gasp and take five steps away from this woman if she was the wife of the Brandon I was thinking of. I took a breath and made the snap decision to stay and pry a little. If she was Brandon's wife, she might be able to help me.

"It's very nice to meet you," I said, hopping onto the stool beside her. "My fiancé, Vito Gerardo, he was Brandon's boss, so I know Brandon."

She gasped. "Get out of town! What a small world!"

I nodded as I waved over a bartender. "That must be exciting, married to the boss of a big firm on Wall Street. Do you guys do a lot of appearances together?" I turned away to look over the menu on the wall, just to look away from her. I needed to hide the pure shock washing over me as I realized she had no idea what kind of business Brandon was actually involved in.

"Actually," I said, "I worked with Brandon for a while. My fiancé is giving me part of his business as a wedding gift, so we'll be co-owners."

"Goodness, so you're not just a pretty face." She leaned forward and laughed.

I forced a laugh too. "Unfortunately, no. I'm out there every day, working. Do you work?"

She sighed. "No, at least not for now. Brandon doesn't want me working, but I told him after the baby I want to start working. I get so tired of being trapped inside all day. It's fine for now, but I want to get out more. At least work a part time job."

"I see. Maybe he's just being protective with the baby and all."

"Well," she paused a moment to sip some soda, "sorry, this pregnancy has me so thirsty."

"Is this your first?" I asked as a bartender came over.

"Yes and no." Her eyes fell.

I studied her for a moment before turning to order with the bartender. "Just a cola, whatever kind you have."

He nodded and grabbed a glass to fill it with ice. As he streamed soda into the cup, I finally said, "I didn't mean to pry, I was just trying to make conversation."

She waved a hand at me. "Oh no! I'm just being overly sensitive. Our family is mixed. Brandon had a son before he met me. His mother died during childbirth, so I'm the only person the boy knows as his mother. His first year or so was spent mostly just with Brandon until we met. Ever since then, I've been mom of the year for Brandon Junior."

"There you are." The bartender set my glass on a coaster, pulling my attention from Alex. I pitied her as I sat there, knowing just how much of a double life Brandon was living. I wanted to scream or cry, I wasn't sure. Possibly both. But I had to stay focused.

I sipped my cola and said, "My fiancé talks about BJ a little, he remembers when he was born."

She lit up. "Does he? That's wonderful to hear."

I nodded, stirring the glass, wondering what to say when she blurted out, "I'm sorry, you seem like such a nice girl. Would you mind getting coffee with me sometime? I know we just met, but I literally have no friends. I knew a few people, but I'm home most of the day. Having somewhere to go would just be great."

The pity in my heart was overwhelming, so I agreed. "Coffee is good. Maybe sometime you can come by Brandon's old work place."

"Really? That would be so great! Maybe I could meet some of his colleagues and old friends like Tim. He's running for mayor, and I had no idea Brandon knew someone running for mayor. That's so exciting."

"I'm sorry," I spoke over her, "Tim Walters—the man running for mayor—knows Brandon, your husband?"

She looked surprised as she nodded slowly and said, "Apparently, they're close. Brandon said he goes to visit Tim's wife in the hospital because she's so sick. So, I told Tim I'd get the information from Brandon to go visit her sometime."

I gripped the counter, hoping that I wouldn't fall over. "Tim Walters," I started, "he's my father. I just never heard him or Brandon mention each other before."

"Oh, you did say your last name was Walters. So that means, the woman in the hospital—"

"Is my mother," I said flatly.

"I'm so sorry," she said quietly.

I stood to my feet and looked over at her. "Alex, I want you to meet me for coffee on Monday at nine in the morning at Gio's diner. Do you know where that is?"

She nodded and I said, "Do not tell Brandon that you talked to me or that you're going to meet me."

"Is it because of his new boss?" she asked.

"It's because your life can be in danger if he knows. Brandon isn't living the life you think he is. I'll tell you what you need to know when you come for coffee. Until then, don't say a word about me." I moved from the bar before she could even speak, and left to find Vito or my dad, whichever I ran into first. But I bumped into Hardy who was talking closely with a woman.

"Excuse me," I said as I stepped forward.

The woman looked over at me and Hardy turned and smiled. "Hey, this is Iyana. I work for her."

The woman nodded, and I couldn't help but notice how beautiful she was. Her skin was as dark as coal, but she was illuminating like a light. She extended a hand to me and said, "My name's Andor. Your guard here was just telling me about how wonderful you are."

I took her hand. "Hardy's a very sweet guy."

"Indeed, he is. Well, I'm going to take my leave now. Don't be a stranger, Hardy, you have my number."

He waved as she stepped away, disappearing into the crowd. "Andor is gorgeous," he said as he looked over at me.

"Walk with me." I turned on my heel but stopped in place when I found Jewels standing still in the crowd. She was staring off, and when I traced her line of vision, I found what she was looking at.

Brandon had gathered his wife and was walking arm in arm with her as they approached a table. They looked like the happiest people in the world, and it almost bothered me because I didn't know if Alex had completely written off what I said, or if she was just a very good actress.

I shook the thoughts away, and when I turned to speak to Hardy, he'd spotted Brandon too, but his focus was on Jewels.

"I need you to get her before she makes a scene. Take her back to the Tower, Hardy, please," I said, grabbing his suit jacket. He looked down at me and nodded, moving to her side.

I turned away and continued my search for Vito until I walked right into him.

"Hey!" he exclaimed. His cheeks were peachy, and his eyes were brighter than ever.

Vito was drunk.

"Vito, you cannot be drunk," I whispered as I grabbed his arm.

"Baby, give me a kiss. I've been wanting to kiss you all night. In fact," he said loudly, "I want to—" I stepped to him and kissed him, drawing an applause and whistles from the onlooking crowd. Before dropping from my tiptoes, I pulled from his lips and whispered in his ear, "If you stay quiet for me, I'll give you whatever you want when we get home."

He groaned, and his hands slid up my back. "What if I can't

wait until then?"

"Then you'll be in trouble."

"I like trouble. You're trouble. You're the only trouble I want to get in." He smirked and shoved me against the nearby table. He was speaking sluggishly into my ear, his hands were racing over my frame, and there was a growing crowd moving around us.

"Tonight," I whispered, "please behave for me." I pulled back and clumsily grabbed the empty glass on the table.

Vito stumbled back, and I began yelling loudly as I tapped the glass with a spoon, "Excuse me! Excuse me!" People in the crowd were already watching Vito and me. They were completely intrigued by Vito's drunken attempt to sleep with me right here in the open.

I cleared my throat and began, "My name is Iyana Walters, daughter of Tim Walters, and I would like to announce today, that Vito and I are getting married."

Gasps and applause rang out and, thankfully, Leo made it to the front of the crowd. I passed him a worried look as the celebration continued, and he nodded.

"We haven't picked a date yet," I continued as I watched Leo pull his phone out. "However, we are planning for a January wedding."

"Impatient, aren't we!" someone yelled from the back and earned a crowd full of laughter.

I nodded politely as I looked around the faces of the room. Some were smiling, others were simply nodding along. Of course, there were some disappointed and angry, but nothing beat the pure look of shock on Brandon's face as he moved to the front without Alex. He eyed me, making me realize it was the first time I'd seen Brandon in a week or so.

I grabbed Vito's hand and pulled him forward.

"I will be serving as—" the lights suddenly shut off, and everyone began to shuffle around and ask questions.

This was my cue to get out of here.

Vito moved, pulling me into him for a kiss. His hands groped me over, and he whispered lustfully, "I've been wanting this since I fell in love with you."

I wanted to fight, but I froze. It was not the time for Vito to be making my heart throb with people moving around in the darkness, and my mind still spinning from the conversations with my father and Alex.

"Iyana! I'm here!" Logan called over my shoulder. I pulled away from Vito, gasping for air, relieved that this night was nearly over.

"He's drunk," I felt in the darkness for Logan. When I placed a hand on his chest, he took it and said, "Let's go."

21

The Gold Rush

Logan walked into the dining room and sat beside me. I stirred in my seat, happy to finally see someone. I hadn't been around anyone since the previous night; as soon as we got in, Logan took Vito to the penthouse, and I stayed here in Vito's place. Hardy was supposed to stay in mine while Jewels was guarded by Rion, but Hardy probably spent the night with Jewels.

Logan pulled out a chair and sat in it before looking over at me. He looked tired, and equally worried. I made the announcement last night, and we'd been getting phone calls all morning.

"Have you returned any calls yet, Iyana?"

I shook my head. "I'm waiting to talk to Vito."

Logan nodded and stretched out onto the table. "I stayed up all night making sure Vito didn't come down here through the night." He raised his head with a grin. "He really likes you."

I pushed his head back onto the table as he chuckled. "Vito said things he doesn't remember."

"Doesn't mean he didn't mean them."

"It was the alcohol talking."

"No." Logan sat up. "The alcohol got him talking, what he said was real."

I tsked him but he shrugged.

"I'm just saying, he got really personal last night. He said some things I never expected him to say."

"What did he say?" I tried to act nonchalant but that only made Logan tease me even more.

"Which do you want to hear? How he fell in love with you before he knew it, or how insanely gorgeous you are to him?"

The door opened before I could answer, and Hardy came in with Kat and Leo. I stood from the table to hug and greet Kat.

"How are you?" she asked as I stepped from the embrace.

"Tired mostly, but I know Vito and I have a lot more work to do today."

She reached into her pocket and pulled out a little notepad. "Well, I've got some good news. In the past two hours, we've received eight dozen bundles of roses, three different fruit baskets, and a few more baskets of assortments." She grinned. "And those are just congratulatory gifts. We'll be getting those all week, and we'll be getting people sending in gifts of good measure."

I was trying not to beam with excitement. Although I was

marrying into a gang society, I was still getting married, and the idea excited me. "What are gifts of good measure?"

"They're support from old clients which tells us they're still willing to work with us. And from new clients, they're security gifts, symbolic of starting business with BT in the hopes of investing in whatever this marriage is bringing together."

"But I didn't even announce what we'd be offering."

"Doesn't matter for a guy at Vito's level," Leo chimed in. "If the Prince of New York is getting married openly, then that means the woman he's chosen is bringing something good to the table. Something that no one else has. Something that you'll want to be the first to invest in before fakes and others try to jump in."

I nodded slowly. The importance of making whatever product Vito wanted to offer worth the investment would rest on my shoulders since I'm the one he's marrying. Which meant, if things went wrong, Vito could say it was a bad deal, and he wouldn't take the fall. He'd still be able to salvage whatever he could while gaining pity from everyone and bringing in even more business.

I sighed, dropping my head into my hands.

"I guess you understand now how important this marriage is," Kat said as she flipped a page on her pad.

"It just seems like Vito's saving himself," I said with a glower.

Logan patted my shoulder. "He has to secure himself. But it's not because he's dangling you out before the sharks, it's because he's trying to make sure if things go wrong with this marriage, BT will remain standing. And you'll be safe."

I shrugged. "I guess so." I had no reason to pity myself since I knew that Vito understood this marriage would literally be the death of BT. Any effort he made to save it would be a waste, but not trying at all would put us in an impossible situation with everyone watching.

Hardy grabbed a seat at the table as he passed me a look. He was trying to hide the worry. But, of course, he wasn't worried for my wellbeing, or even for BT, the only thing Hardy was concerned with, or rather the only *person*, was Jewels.

The defeat in his eyes spoke to the lack of conversation between the two of them last night. But he knew being here right now was not about gathering information about Jewels. He was still my guard, and his loyalty remained with BT. He took a breath and nodded at me, his boyish smile returning as he pushed away the thoughts of Jewels.

In some ways, Hardy was still very young, and very immature. But then, there were these moments, when I could see him visibly putting his best foot forward, and it seemed like he wasn't so young at all. Like he might understand more than I give him credit for.

I nodded, giving him a small smile as I looked over at the door. It opened to reveal a very tired Vito. He was back in his usual sweatpants and a big shirt, but he wore a hat to try to shield his face so we wouldn't see how exhausted he was. Or maybe he was embarrassed.

He cleared his throat and strolled to the table, hand in pocket, the other swaying beside him. He stopped in front of me and leaned over to peck my head, "Good morning," he whispered into my hair.

I closed my eyes and whispered a 'good morning' back. He stepped away and sat beside me at the head of the table. "Where's Rion?"

"On post. I've gathered information from him," Kat said as she waved her notepad.

"Fine. Everyone, take a seat."

As everyone moved to follow his orders, I asked, "Would you like some coffee, Vito? I know you hate it, but it might make you feel less sluggish."

He nodded. "Coffee would be perfect."

As I stood, he caught my hand, raising his head to look up at me. My hungover fiancé looked bleary as he blinked. "You're not my secretary anymore." His eyes slid over to Logan. "Coffee, with three shots of espresso. Black."

Logan rolled his eyes and left the table for the kitchen as I took my seat again.

"Now," Vito said, "we need to talk about last night."

"What do you remember?" Leo asked.

Hardy chuckled, but when he noticed no one else laughing, he cleared his throat and started, "Actually, I'd like to start with something."

"What?" Vito said flatly.

"A man spilled his drink on me by accident, and we ended up having a conversation. He told me he was here networking, looking for some suppliers for his new cannabis store he was opening in three weeks."

"Isn't it a little late to be looking for a supplier if he's already set to open?" Leo asked.

Hardy nodded. "I thought the same thing, until he said his supplier pulled out at the last minute, and he's been left with nothing."

Vito shifted in his seat. "Who was the supplier?"

"Dale," Hardy said.

"That's a higher level than the man lost." Vito tapped his finger on the table.

"This is Brandon's doing," Logan said as he walked in with Vito's coffee.

I glanced around the table, taking in the distraught faces around me. I knew I didn't know much, but I hated to be the only person who didn't understand what had taken place.

Kat noticed my confusion and cleared her throat to catch my attention. "Brandon took Dale for the life of that low level Grizzly, so now what? What's going to be our move?"

I nodded slowly, thanking Kat for inconspicuously bringing me up to speed.

"That's the tricky part about politics." Vito slurped his coffee. "You don't always know who belongs to who. Grizzly has the upper hand because Brandon has serviced both of us. However, we know about Brandon's warehouse, and they don't know about our new business."

"What is the new business, exactly?" Leo asked.

Vito glanced over at me lazily and nodded.

Finally, I thought, *I can be of use.*

"Vito's new business is actually two businesses."

"Two?" Hardy questioned.

"Yes." I nodded. "Two businesses. An animal clinic, and a jewelry store called, 'The Ice Rink.'"

"Alright." Logan shrugged. "What's the point of them?"

"The animal clinic serves as a means of building new partnerships with dog breeders. They make a lot of money. They'll pay us to do evaluations, checkups, and shots before the dog is adopted. We are then the recognized clinic for these clients with puppies. We'll also have a training program to turn these puppies into guard dogs."

I was cheerful when I explained it, but as I watched everyone's reaction, the cheer sank into uncertainty.

"V, you can't be serious, right?" Leo folded his arms, an incredulous look on his face. "An animal clinic? Do you want the world to know you actually like this girl? You're doing this for her not for BT."

Vito slurped his coffee again and set his cup down on the table. He glanced over at me, his eyes barely visible beneath the visor of his hat. After a moment, he took my hand and held it. I didn't know what to expect or what to say, and I didn't know what Vito was going to say or do.

He looked over at Leo, and then he looked at everyone. "If anyone has a problem with my leadership they can leave, because the next person who questions what I do for my fiancé will be killed. I am the leader of BT, and I'm going to be a husband, which means BT will always take a backseat to my wife. But it will also always be *connected* to her. One effects the other." He took a breath. "The clinic is for Iyana. I want her to be able to practice as a veterinarian, however, the clinic will also act as a safe."

He stood and began to pace the floor. Everyone watched him as the coffee worked its black magic and pulled Vito out of his morning slump.

"As we speak, the space I purchased is being gutted and remolded. Stacks of money are being used to fill statues, walls, and floors, and I've brought enough pure silver and gold to be used as medical instruments."

"Incredible." Kat gleamed. "How'd you pull that off?"

"I invested in a lot of things when I first took my place here as the head of BT," Vito explained. "I had a clinic built for my mother. At the time, when she was recovering, she loved the recovery animals that would come and visit her in the hospital. So I started a clinic here in New York for her, and a sanctuary in California."

I remembered when Vito first proposed the idea on the flight home. He told me he liked the thought of a clinic just for me; it would be a safe place for me to work because he was going to open it to civilians.

Gangs follow one code: Don't get civilians involved. If they do, like how Vito took me in, the civilian becomes your liability. But gangs are allowed to interact with civilians as long as they don't end up finding something out that they shouldn't. Civilians also provided a sense of protection. Most gangs won't attack a place frequented by innocents, unless provoked.

That's why this clinic would be the perfect safe, no one would suspect a business open to civilians was actually the safe itself. Every gang had a safe—its hidden location depended on how clever the one hiding things is.

"How sweet." Kat pressed her hand to her chest, but Logan interjected with a snort, "Real cute, Vee. But what about The Ice Rink?"

"The Ice Rink is where transactions will be happening. We're selling gold—*bars* of gold, and diamonds," I said.

"We're selling twenty-four karats, and Malawi," Vito announced.

Logan erupted to his feet and stared at Vito. "You got your hands on Malawi?"

Vito chuckled. "I've got my own field across fifty acres of land. The other fifty is for the crew I hired to take care of the gold, off the record of course."

Logan fell back into his seat, quiet and stumped. "We're going to win this war, aren't we?"

Vito smiled. "I never intended to lose."

22

More Lies

"Morning, Brandon," Alex said groggily.

I sat on the edge of the bed and stepped into my shoes. Last night went totally wrong. All of the Pack was there, and now Vito's marrying Iyana. Which means they probably have the Abletons back. What else could she bring to the table besides them?

"Brandon?" Alex cooed.

"What?" I snapped.

She retracted the hand she'd been using to reach across the bed. I didn't have time for her. I didn't have time for any of this. I needed to start making moves now. *I need to bring something to Grizzly before word gets to him about Vito and...* My thoughts froze as my phone hummed. I stopped tying my boot and stared at the phone.

With a deep breath, I picked it up, thanking God it was only Jewels. I declined her call and finished tying my boots.

"I don't know when I'll be back," I said as I stood from the bed, "so don't wait up for me."

"What does that mean? A day, three days, a year?" she snapped.

I whirled around and she sank deeper into the bed, bulging eyes turning soft and apologetic.

"I'm sorry, Brandon," she said. "I'm just a little tired from all the walking around last night."

"That's why I don't want to take you out while you're pregnant," I said as I began to tie my tie. "Your hormones get out of whack, and you start acting crazy."

"I know," she muttered. "I'm sorry."

I sighed and shrugged. "I'll see you." I didn't turn back to hug or kiss her. I left Alex in the bed and headed down the stairs and out the door.

In a brewing silence, I drove over to the warehouse where Dahodda and Brooke were standing guard—this time with no blunts.

"Morning, Brandon," Brooke said as he opened the door to the warehouse for me.

"Have we had anyone come by? Any reports? Anything?"

"Someone called and said they tried musing over the Stalls, but they couldn't after last night."

I swore loudly and barked, "It's the Stolls, you idiot! And that was a huge opportunity we missed!" I slammed my hands onto the table holding some of our products and they collapsed to the floor. After the clattering, I took a breath and asked, "Does anyone have any positive news?"

"Jewels called. Said it was urgent," Dahodda said nervously.

"Get her on the phone. I want her here in minutes. If you have to go get her, I don't care, just get her here now."

"Understood," they said in unison.

"Wait—Brooke, you call Jewels and stand guard. Dahodda, you clean this mess up. Don't bother me unless it's Jewels."

I went to my desk and sat down, staring at the papers in front of me, wondering if this was it for me. I didn't want it to be. I'd done so much work, stealing from BT, stealing from Grizzly. All to get me to the top of Gang Grizzly. All I wanted was to run my own gang, and I'd done everything right but, somehow, Vito got everything. Even his father's worst accounts were turned around for him. He was handed a wonderful life while I've struggled to be more than a wingman.

"I will have Gang Grizzly. I will be the next Grizzly."

I closed my eyes and took a deep breath. I knew I'd betrayed a lot of people and had hurt many others, but in the long run, it would be for the better. That's what I remind myself every day, that this is for the good of New York.

We don't need a pampered prince who's had everything handed to him. New York thinks they need someone like Grizzly who can rise from a handful of hope. But New York needs me. Someone who's been nothing all their life and didn't even have hope that they would ever become something.

I'd been second all my life. I was the second brother, the

second in command, the second at everything. But it was time for more than being second, I needed to be number one. I deserved to be number one.

When I joined BT, I was trying to get my father to notice me, but he ended up despising me for joining a gang. He clung to my oldest brother like he'd always done and gave him everything. He wrote me out of his will and his life, and I was forced to make a living at BT. I didn't want to, initially, but when Mr. Gerardo took me under his wing, when he noticed me, I thought he'd be proud of me. I thought I'd finally found a father, someone who would make me number one, but I found out he had a son, and things changed.

When I tried to get a rival gang to attack BT during Mr. Gerardo's time, things went wrong. Mrs. Gerardo was not the target, but Fernando, the leader of a little Spanish gang that was making a name for itself, was obsessed with her. When I gave him the information on the Gerardos, he went for her instead of Vito because he didn't want anyone to have her except himself.

He almost killed Mrs. Gerardo, which sent Tobias into a turbulent downward spiral. Mr. Gerardo wanted to step down, and when talks of another heir came up, talks of a peace offering, my name wasn't passed around. In fact, I was asked to be the one who helped his son make a name for himself, just like I'd helped Mr. Gerardo. I would've been the perfect offering, and that had been my plan, to bring Fernando's gang and BT together. But I was overlooked, yet again.

"Brandon?" Dahodda called.

I blinked out of my thoughts and floated into reality. "What?"

"Jewels is here."

"Send her in," I said.

I glanced at all the photos of Jewels and me on my desk. She was the only one who believed in me. She was the only one who believed I could be the leader of a gang. That's why, if I could make things work out, I'm going to leave Alex and marry Jewels. She's the one I truly loved.

I watched her as she approached my desk. She was beautiful and radiant, and I wanted her all to myself. I couldn't stand the thought of Hardy's hands, or any other man's hands, on her. She was mine, and mine alone.

"I've been trying to reach you," she said as she dropped her purse on my desk for an embrace.

"I'm sorry," I said. "How'd you get away?"

"Rion let me go, but I've only got an hour."

"Why'd he let you go?"

"Does it matter? I'm here," she said forcefully.

"It does matter," I said, grabbing her by the waist. "You know how I feel about other men touching you."

"Not all men touch me." She pushed me away. "Rion's actually nice."

"Nicer than me? You like him more than me?"

She shook her head. "Brandon, can I please just tell you what I need to?"

"Not until you tell me there's no one but me."

"There's never been anyone but you. We have a child

together, Brandon, I love you."

"And Hardy? You love him?"

"He's a child. I don't love him, he's just there."

"Get rid of him," I said as I went back to my seat.

"Fine. Done."

"What was so urgent that you called me this morning?"

Her face sank into a tight frown. She was carefully choosing her words, and I knew something was wrong. Jewels was carefree, she said whatever she wanted, unafraid of the consequences. She'd been hardened by the harsh reality of being a brothel worker. People always thought less of her because she was paid for sex, and she normally looked like she was some type of sex fiend. Everyone liked the way she looked until she made them angry, then she was reduced to just a whore, or worse. It stopped bothering her a long time ago, now she basks in her sensuality.

"Brandon," she said without looking at me, "who was that woman from last night?"

"What woman?" I tried to play it off. I didn't know she'd seen me with Alex.

"The pregnant one. Who is she?"

"My cousin."

"Don't lie to me," she said hotly. Her eyes were burning through me now, but I couldn't tell her the truth. I'd lose her, and I couldn't afford that. She was all I had, despite the way Alex could make me feel, I believed that if I gave Jewels the time and attention, she'd make me feel even better than my wife.

"Jewels," I stood up and grabbed her hand, "I'm not lying. I needed a date, and she'd been fighting with her husband and wanted to get out the house. That's all."

She eyed me, but only nodded. I tried not to let her see my relief as I exhaled slowly. "Listen," I said, still holding her hands, "I'm going to need your help."

"With what?"

"With getting into the pockets of everyone on this list." I pulled a sticky note from my desk and passed it to her.

"Pockets or pants?"

"Jewels, come on."

"No." She extended the paper back to me. "I'm tired of doing this. How about you sleep with their wives or something? Maybe that'll change their minds."

"Stop it," I growled. "We need this."

"We?" she shouted. "When has any of this ever been for me? This has all been for you, and I don't even know why I do it." She shook her head. "I don't even know why I love you."

"Excuse me?" I snatched her by the arm, but she didn't fight. The loneliness in her eyes almost made me weak. *Have I been the reason behind her unhappiness all along?*

"What are you going to do? Beat me?" She shrugged. "Fine. Hit me, then. Cut me. Hurt me. Do whatever. They've all done it before. Every time I show a little self-respect, everyone wants to beat me down—like I'm not allowed to think highly of myself. To have a little dignity. What's holding you back?" she seethed. "Nothing stopped you the last time."

I shoved her away, and she tripped to the floor. "I was

wrong about you," I said as I grabbed my jacket off my chair. "I thought things between us were solid. But I guess this is all just a game for you. Get those names on my side, and we're through."

"Now we're through? After everything?"

I leaned down and said, "If you want things to stay the same, then get me in a room with these men, ready to sign a deal." I stood up straight and walked out the warehouse without her. She was making me change my mind about leaving Alex for her, but Jewels always came around. I could trust that she'd make things happen.

As I got in my truck, I got a phone call from Grizzly. I wanted to decline, but I knew the minute my finger pushed the button my head would be blown off.

Begrudgingly, I answered, "Hello?"

"If you're not here in five minutes, I'm going to kill you."

"I'll be there soon. I'm getting on the highway now."

"Why did you make me have to make this phone call?"

"I haven't been out the house. I'm just now leaving for the day. I had a late night."

"Good," he said smugly, "then I'm expecting you to bring me a silver platter with new accounts."

The phone went dead, and I hurled it into the seat. Beating the steering wheel, I screamed. I screamed so loud and hard I began to choke. But even then, I still screamed, hoping the pain in my throat would be my own punishment. I was a fool to let my guard down at BT, now they're moving on without me, as if I don't have information on them.

How could they move so confidently with me holding their gang by threads? I could have all their accounts in an instant. Make their clients think they've got no security. I gripped the steering wheel as thoughts of Iyana filled my head.

"She's too smart for her own good," I said sharply. Vito was smart, but he's probably banking on using her for something explosive. I've got to break her and tear down Vito and BT.

I reached over and grabbed my phone and dialed a number.

"Hello and thank you for calling St. Sessa—"

"Cut the crap, Jill."

A girly voice giggled on the other end. "What can I do for you, Brandon?"

"Pull the plug on January first. Don't tell anyone, and if visitors come, tell them Mr. Walter has stopped public visitations."

She didn't speak for a moment, and then her small voice came, "Are you sure?"

"Yes," I answered quickly. "And, Jill?"

"Yes?"

"Don't tell Tim either, not until he comes to visit after the first."

"Of course."

I pulled into Grizzly's cove and went inside. Every step was more dreadful than the last, heavier than the last, more anxious than the last. I could barely hold myself together, as I knew I was walking into a minefield. One wrong word to Grizzly and

I'd be killed. I thought about coming in and killing him first on the drive over, but I didn't know if I'd walk out alive, and the whole point of killing Grizzly was so that I could take his seat, not die trying.

As the double doors opened to his lair, I walked inside to find him sitting on his couch getting a massage by a woman only wearing a thong and pasties.

"I'll make this quick, because I don't want to hear your explanations," he said with his bulky dark arms crossed against his chest.

"I'm giving you two weeks to make things right. Bring me accounts and the Abletons. I want both. If you don't deliver both, well…" He chuckled nonchalantly. "Just make sure you bring me both in two weeks."

"You can't be serious?" I complained.

"I am!" he shouted as he stood quickly from the couch. "I am serious because I am sick of the lies. You told me that girl Vito's marrying was our key to finding the Abletons. But she's running around here about to marry the Prince of the City!"

"I know what it looks like, but if you'd just let me—"

"No! Just nothing!" He crossed the room in big heavy steps and towered over me. He leaned down to snarl in my ear, "I will have you stripped, beaten, and enjoyed by each one of my men right in front of that pregnant wench of yours. Do you understand me?"

I swallowed thickly, trying not to look panicked. "Yes."

"Good." He stood upright and patted my shoulder, and it seemed as if the old wrinkly man had returned to his normal height, which was only two or three inches taller than me.

"I suspect you won't need any help. You can do this on your own, right?" He chuckled as he walked back to his couch. He wasn't expecting me to return with anything, that's why he wouldn't help me. But I would prove him wrong.

"Yes, I can."

"Very good." He sat back down into the woman's bosom and waved a hand. "You're dismissed."

23

One of Us

"Malawi Gold," Hardy said as we drove down the street, "that's some rare weed."

"So I've heard," I said, staring out the window.

Since Vito revealed he had a gold farm, Logan, Hardy, and Leo have been driving me up the wall about going to see the fields and trying the product. Both of which I have denied.

"I know." Hardy pulled into the parking lot of the diner. "You're tired of hearing us talk about the gold rush, but this is some good Kush, Iyana."

I tried to hold in the exaggerated sigh I wanted to blow out, settling for a roll of my eyes as I continued to stare out the window. I'd been counting the trees that passed, every single one was another apology Vito kept issuing to me for having to survive the rest of the black-tie event without him since he'd been drunk.

"It's so good that it causes—"

"Have you ever had it?"

He slapped a hand to the passenger seat as he looked over his shoulder. "No." The car moved slowly as he backed us into a spot.

I said, "Then you have no idea what you're talking about."

"Why are we even here?"

I watched out the window as a car pulled up across the lot. Alex stepped out and glanced around before ducking her head as she walked into the diner.

"That woman," Hardy whispered.

"I'm here to see her." I opened my door and hopped out the truck. Hardy came around the front and grabbed my arm.

"Are you sure this is a good idea?"

I snatched my arm away. "Are you asking for Jewels's sake or the Pack's?"

He didn't answer, but I didn't bother waiting for one either. Opening the door, I stepped inside and greeted Emilia at the front counter.

"Where's Vito?" she said as she smacked her gum.

"He couldn't be here," I told her.

She smirked as she moved to grab a coffee pot. "He couldn't be here, or he shouldn't be here?" I palmed my neck nervously, but she waved a hand. "There are things that a woman can handle better than a man." She winked and I exhaled deeply as I nodded.

I found Alex sitting in a booth drinking a chocolate shake.

I waved Hardy off as I went over and sat across from her. "You're here," she gasped.

"You sound surprised."

"I didn't know what to expect."

"You should've expected me to tell you the truth."

She swallowed, dropping her eyes back to her shake. "Why has he been lying to me?"

"Do you have a picture of your son?"

She nodded as she grabbed her purse and pulled out her phone. "This is little BJ."

He had light brown skin like Jewels but kept his father's face.

I dug into my pocket and set a picture on the table. Alex looked at it before slowly lifting it to look closer.

"She had a similar reaction when she saw you," I said.

Alex covered her mouth, her chest rising and falling rapidly. "Saw me?"

"At the event last week."

"She was there?"

I nodded. "She is very much alive and well. One of our best workers."

The picture trembled in her hand as she whispered, "She works at the firm too?"

"No." I shook my head. "She works at the brothel I co-own. It helps us discover clients for our drug trades."

She looked up at me for the first time since receiving the picture. "What did you just say?"

"That your husband has been involved with a sex worker

for the past six years, and he's been in the drug business all his working life."

Alex squinted and lowered the picture. "I don't believe you." Her nose had turned red, and her cheeks were flush. "I don't believe you. I almost did. Showing me this photo of a woman who looks...." Her voice trailed off as her mouth began to tremble and her words would not come. "You're telling me," she whispered aggressively, "that my husband is some kind of drug dealer?"

I leaned across the table and grabbed her hands. "Alex, I need you to trust me." I reached into my pocket and placed a card in her hand. As she looked it over, I explained, "Go home and search every pocket, every article of clothing, every room, all your vehicles for a card like this. You'll find one. And when you do, I want you to give me a call."

"IncogVito's Diamonds," she whispered as she set the card down. She dug through her purse again and retrieved her wallet. From it, she pulled out a card identical to the one I'd just given her.

"I found this in his pants pocket a year ago, and I never knew what it was. I've looked it up online, and nothing came up. I thought it was just a jewelry store. I found it around Valentine's Day when Brandon bought me a beautiful necklace."

"You thought it was from here."

She nodded.

"IncogVito's Diamonds is a brothel. It's where Brandon met that woman in the picture."

She slapped a hand over her mouth and began to gag behind it. Scooting out the booth, she raced for the bathroom. I caught Hardy's eye as I stood from the booth to follow her.

"Alex," I said as I walked the stalls of the women's restroom.

She flushed the toilet and emerged from the last stall. "That chocolate shake, I told myself not to get one." She tried to chuckle but instead, she fell into me, bursting into tears. "How could he do this to me!?"

"Alex, you cannot cry right now," I said stiffly.

My heart broke for her, but I needed her head clear so I could get any leads from her. I wanted information for BT, but I needed information about my father and mother. I hadn't told anyone I'd spoken with him at the event, I decided I'd wait to tell Vito because it seemed like with our announcement, things began to change rapidly. We had to move our wedding up to the day after New Year's. The sooner Vito and I got married, the sooner we could start taking investors and clients. We didn't want to take them before getting married since our marriage was the entire reason clients believe we're rolling out new products.

"How can I not cry!? My husband—" she whimpered.

"Listen to me," I grabbed her shoulders, "in two weeks I'll be married. Which means all you have to do is not mention any of this for another fourteen days."

"You expect me to go home and not utter a word about this?"

"He will kill you or get BJ involved."

She gasped.

"After two weeks, you need to give me a call. My number's on the back of that card. Call me because things will get hectic, and I'll have somewhere safe for you and BJ to stay."

"You mean," she stepped back, "you want me to leave Brandon?"

"I want you to be safe and not caught in the crossfire of all this."

Reluctantly, she nodded.

I told her, "Wait at least two weeks. Then call. Got it?"

"Got it."

We left the bathroom and went our separate ways. When I got into the truck again with Hardy, he sat in the front without starting the car.

"Hardy, let's go," I pestered.

"Are you going to tell Vito?"

"If you'd ever get me home, I could."

"Why didn't you tell him before the meeting?"

"Because I didn't want him to try and stop me, and we needed this meeting to be as low profile as possible. If Vito knew, he would've sent a wagon of guards which would've scared Alex away."

"You're dealing with a man's wife, Iyana. Anything goes wrong with her, BT is going down the drain." He was watching me in the rearview mirror, but I looked off at the diner through the window.

"If something happens to Alex, then we have Brandon in a position he can't get out of. She's valuable to him, he won't risk it."

Hardy adjusted in his seat to look at me. "And what if he doesn't value her as much you think? What happens to her then?"

"But she is valuable to—"

"But what if she's not!"

"Then nothing's lost!"

He gasped, and there was a mist filling his eyes, but it only made me angry.

"We'll be right back where we started," I said calmly. "Nothing on Brandon, just caught in a war with him."

"Do you even hear yourself? How could you let someone be dragged into this the same way we were?"

"You really think I would bring her into this after everything I've been through? You really think I have no plan for her and her children's lives? Hardy, there's a whole society operating New York City and beyond that no one knows about! You don't know who's involved with what, so her life was in danger the very day she stepped foot into that event last week."

Silence fell over us as we sat in the stinging moment. Hardy turned back in his seat and started the engine.

"I didn't know you were trying to protect her," he said as he pulled off.

"I needed to gain her trust." I sighed. "That's why we met today."

"I'm sorry," he said stiffly.

"Me too."

He raised a brow and glanced into the mirror. "For what?"

"For never noticing how much you really wanted to go home. You don't want to be here anymore, but you're like me." I almost chuckled. "You've got no place to go."

We rode in silence the rest of the way to the Tower. When we arrived, Vito was sitting on the couch of my living room, sipping orange juice.

"Where were you all morning?" he said as Hardy sat beside him.

I took my jacket off and hung it in my closet as I called over my shoulder, "I had a meeting."

"With who? And why didn't you tell me?"

"I needed to do this on my own," I said as I emerged from the closet.

Vito was standing now, glaring at me. I knew he'd be mad, but I didn't think it would matter that much. "Well?" he snapped. "Say something."

"I went to see Alex."

His face wrinkled. "Who is Alex?"

"Brandon's wife," Hardy said as he drank the rest of Vito's orange juice.

I rolled my eyes, but Vito's had nearly doubled in size as he stood there. He wasn't glaring anymore, he was dumbfounded, absently blinking at me.

"Brandon has a wife?" he asked.

"Yes, and I met with her to talk about Brandon."

"Did you tell her the truth?"

"Yes."

"Why?" He flung his hands open and turned away, shaking his head.

"For good reason, Vito."

He whirled back around and barked, "What is it?"

"Hey, Vee, calm down," Hardy said.

"You don't get it." He looked down at Hardy, and then back at me. "Interfering with someone's personal life can screw BT into the dirt. We're traitors now. You never bring the outside world in for any reason. That's why the gang that tried to kill my mother didn't last, because they were traitors to the society. They're untrustworthy."

"I know, but I thought it was alright because he brought her to the event last week. He brought her into this life, I'm just trying to get us leverage while she's here."

Vito folded his arms across his chest and pondered for a moment. "She was there at the event?"

"Yes, that's where I met her. I didn't know who she was until she asked if I worked with her husband, Brandon Jefferson, at the firm."

"And you're sure she's not just a hooker?"

"She's pregnant," Hardy added.

Vito shot him a look, one that was confused and frustrated. "Pregnant? Why would he do that?"

"I don't know." I shrugged. "But I told her a little about the work we do. Mostly, I told her about Jewels."

"Why?"

"Because I needed her to trust me. I needed her to think I was on her side, which is true, but we need her, and she needs us if she wants to be safe. For all we know, she could be in danger. Someone may have a problem with Brandon that we don't know about and could be targeting her."

Vito ran a hand over his hair as he exhaled deeply.

"It's true." Hardy nodded. "She's a living target right now."

"What if she isn't?" Vito shook his head. "What if no one paid her any attention because she was pregnant, and they never saw her with Brandon? We just put the target on her back."

"How?" I shrugged. "We're helping her."

"You're using her, Iyana! You just said you wanted her to trust you and that she could provide leverage for us." Vito's words were piercing and callous, but also pure and true.

It was easy to fool Hardy, make him believe that I cared about her safety because there was a part of me that did care. But an even bigger part of me wanted information about Brandon's connection to my father and, ultimately, to my mother.

"Hardy," Vito spoke into the silence, "go downstairs and talk to Jewels. We'll be down in five minutes. We need her to tell us everything she knows about Brandon. This woman is in danger if anyone saw you two meeting today." He paused. "Where did you meet?"

"At Gio's," I said.

He closed his eyes slowly and dropped his head. "Hardy, make a call to Logan, tell him to put a perimeter around Gio's for the next week."

Hardy moved from the couch and nodded before brisking

by me and out the door. When the door closed, Vito and I were left in silence.

"Why did you do this, Ana? You don't know this world like I do."

"I know enough," I said curtly.

"What's your problem?"

"My problem is that you're treating me like I just brought chaos to your front door."

"You did." He nodded dramatically and I tsked him.

Turning away, I went to the kitchen. "I can't deal with this right now."

"Iyana," Vito snapped behind me.

I whipped around and snapped back, "What, Vito? What do you want? To tell me how much I screwed up? Again? To embarrass me? What do you want?"

He was squinting, so unsure of my behavior. But I couldn't blame him. Vito and I have never argued, we've barely disagreed, but I've never done anything detrimental before. And, honestly speaking, I've seen Vito kill a man for not following orders—so his anger wasn't so bad or unjustified right now.

I sighed and turned for the kitchen, dragging myself to the counter to lean against it. Vito followed me in and leaned against the fridge.

"I spoke with my father at that event."

"What?"

"He told me something, and so did Alex, that's why I wanted to meet with her. I did want her to know the truth, but

I needed her to trust me for my own benefit."

"Iyana, what did they tell you?"

"My father," I swallowed hard, "he told me he couldn't give me any information about himself or my mother, or why he was running for mayor because he'd be killed. And Alex…" I paused to catch my breath. I hadn't said any of this out loud since the event, and I didn't know how weighty the information truly was.

"Tell me," Vito urged when my pause turned into a simmering silence.

"She said she'd met my father that night, and that my father and Brandon knew each other. She told me they're old friends." I sniffled, feeling a dry lump form in my throat. "And she said Brandon's been going to visit my mother in the hospital."

Vito was silent for a moment. He stared at the floor as he asked, "Are you sure she knew that Brandon and your father are friends?"

I nodded. "Yes. She said she met him at the event."

There was silence for a while. Vito was staring aimlessly at everything but me while I tried to think of a viable explanation for the friendship between Brandon and my father.

"Do you think it's possible we're looking at this the wrong way?"

"What do you mean?"

"From those conversations, do you think Brandon is actually your father's friend or not?"

"I can't believe you would even ask me that." I scowled at

Vito, but he wasn't fazed.

"I wanted to ask because once we start down this road, there's no going back. Blood is going to be spilled, and this war isn't going to be so political anymore."

"Why? What has to change because of this?"

"We're going to need to take Brandon's wife as leverage against him. He's not going to let your father go, not if he really is behind him running for mayor."

I covered my mouth, and Vito looked at me with an apology in his eyes, like there was more he should say but couldn't. He didn't have to say anything more. His warning was loud and clear. A life for a life.

If we wanted my father back, we'd have to gamble Alex's life for it. And if something went wrong, I could lose both my parents and get an innocent woman and her children killed. But, in two weeks, I was going to be the new leader of BT. I needed to be ready to make these kinds of decisions. I needed to be able to make the decision between what's important to me and what was important for BT. They needed to overlap and be the same.

I gritted my teeth and clutched my hand into a fist. No matter how hard I tried, what was important to me, and what was important for BT were not overlapping. The personal life of a gang member wasn't meant to be messed with because we weren't supposed to bring civilians into gang affiliations. Despite how often that line was crossed, how often families were torn apart, and gangs lost their trust and fought for it back, I didn't want BT to be known for that as it dissipated.

But there was a war within me because I didn't know what else to do.

If we took Alex as leverage, we'd risk becoming traitors. But if I didn't get more information out of her, I wouldn't learn anything about my father.

"Iyana…"

I looked up from the floor at the sound of my name. Vito had crossed the room and was standing right in front of me now. He lifted my chin and said, "Let's talk to Jewels first. See what we can get out of her and go from there. There's no need to rush into this decision, because I'm going to do what I must to rescue your mother." He took my hands and let his eyes slowly raise to mine. "But I want you to know that whatever you decide, I'm going to use every resource I have to back you up."

"Thank you," I whispered as I sank my head into his chest. Before I could relax against him, a knock came to the door, and when I lifted my head, I noticed that Vito was as confused as me.

"I'll get it," he said as he left the kitchen. I followed slowly and listened as the door opened.

"Where is she?" Jewels snapped.

"I tried to stop her!" Hardy cried behind her.

"Where is who?" Vito asked over Hardy's whining.

"Where's his pregnant whore! I know you're hiding her!"

"What did you say to her?" Vito snapped.

"I… I—" Hardy was fumbling for words as I rounded the corner and all the confusion stopped. Jewels glared at me, her eyes blazing like actual flames had replaced them.

"You have never liked me!" she shouted as she thrust herself at me.

Vito got in front of her and blocked her flailing, and Hardy grabbed her by the waist to drag her away. But she grabbed the door frame and screeched, "You can't do this to me! You can't let her in here! I'm going to kill her!"

"Hardy, get her out of here!" Vito yelled.

Hardy dragged a flailing and wailing Jewels down the hall, and I watched quietly. Admittedly, I did feel bad for Jewels, she didn't know anything, just like Alex. But was I to blame for all of this?

24

Did You Forget to be Happy?

Christmas and New Year's came with little celebration. Vito and I shared a quiet dinner and exchanged gifts on Christmas. I also spent a little time with Kat, but she told me holidays were the most dangerous time of year since people usually let their guard down. We didn't get to spend much time together, but I was happy to see her. New Year's was similar, except, Hardy and Logan joined Vito and me for the countdown, and I got emotional. I cried because the following day, everything was going to permanently change, and I was overwhelmed.

Vito and I decided I would walk down the aisle, and then spend a maximum of two hours at the reception. He didn't want me around drunk gang members and outsiders, since we couldn't opt for a dry bar like I wanted. Two of BT's longtime clients offered to host the bar in exchange for first pick of his new business endeavors, whatever they thought these endeavors may be. But my mind was preoccupied with thoughts of my parents, thoughts of Alex and Jewels. It was hard to focus in the moment during the past two weeks, but I knew that today I needed to forget everything and try to enjoy the night.

"You look beautiful," Kat said as she fixed the train of my wedding gown.

"I'm so nervous," I said shakily.

In the mirror, I took in my attire. A mermaid white gown fell to the floor in a satin white color. Down my back was a bit of lace that eventually gave way to my flowing train. My strapless gown and short veil were what Kat and I had picked out together. I'd always wanted to get married, but I'd never planned for it, and even if I had, I couldn't have planned for someone to spend millions of dollars on me when I wasn't even sure if Vito and I loved each other, despite what Dafni said.

We felt the same way. Both sharing a strong liking for each other, but I didn't know if it was love or if that even mattered at this point. I was here now, and I had to go through with this no matter if love lived in my heart or not. I just hoped that one day it would.

"I don't know why you're so worried," Kat spoke into my thoughts. "You look stunning, and your bouquet is amazing." She handed me the large arrangement of flowers I'd never even heard of. "And your husband to be is a very handsome man who just happens to believe like you do."

"I know … I just…" I took one more glance at myself, and Kat stepped into the mirror with me. Her hair was down, resting all over her shoulders as her sweetheart neckline plunged into a taupe-colored dress.

"What if this is all wrong?" I said to Kat. "What if I'm not supposed to marry Vito? What if I let this world consume me? And I'm doing something so big without my mother or father." I sniffled. "What if Vito doesn't love me?"

Kat disappeared from the mirror for a second and returned with a tissue. Dabbing my cheeks, she said, "What if this is the right thing to do? What if you are supposed to marry Vito, and this is exactly the plan of God? What if God put you here because you're strong enough not to be consumed by BT? What if it's alright to make decisions without the people closest to you?" She paused and lifted my chin. "And what if Vito does love you? Then everything works out, but that can't be part of God's plan, right? Why on earth would He plan for you to be happy?"

We began to laugh at her sarcasm, and Kat dabbed my cheeks again. "A bride should never cry on her wedding. It's supposed to be one of the happiest days of her life."

I sighed, exhaling all the worry that had begun to suffocate me. "You're right. It's my day today. I should enjoy it, not worry about it."

She nodded. "Besides, I have a feeling you know God's plan better than you're pretending, you're just afraid of making the wrong move. Let Him guide you, Ana," she said as she tossed the tissues into the trash. "God doesn't reveal plans to us so we can move Him off the throne and do it all ourselves. He reveals them to us to deepen our trust and faith in Him to know that no matter the situation, the plan of God will be fulfilled. You've just got to trust Him."

"Ok," I whispered.

I knew God wanted BT to fall, but how He planned on getting there was beyond me. Right now, it seemed like BT was being built up, not torn down, but I'd come this far without questioning God, I figured I could go a little further.

Kat rubbed my arm and took my hands. "Now, go out there, walk the aisle to your husband to be, become his wife, enjoy the party, and get laid."

I gasped and began to laugh giddily. "Why would you say that before I go out?" I whispered at her as she led me to the main doors.

"Because I need you smiling." She flashed me her own big smile and opened the door for me to step through.

I was grateful that Kat was my matron of honor today, she was able to talk some sense into me and keep my head from spinning.

I stood at the double door entrance to the church and took a breath as the piano began to play the entrance song. The grand oak doors opened, revealing a large church with guests I'd never seen before. We didn't have a bridal dinner since the wedding was so close to the holidays and we only had one rehearsal with bridesmaids and groomsmen picked out by Kat and Leo.

My bridesmaids were a fleet of eighteen women and Kat as

the matron of honor. Some were from the brothel and BT, while others were old friends of BT, or the daughters of longtime clients. The groomsmen were the same; members of BT, including Hardy and Leo, sons of old clients (including Gio Jr.), with Logan as Vito's best man.

Jewels didn't come, which was no shock to me. She hadn't come from her room since she'd tried to attack me, not even for the holidays, but Rion's reported activity in her room—crying, screaming, smoking—certified that she was alive and had not escaped. Rion stayed home of course, to watch her.

At the altar, Vito looked like a new man. He looked lean with muscle definition, not bulky like Brandon. His suit looked like it was stitched around every part of his body, perfectly tailored for him. His jacket was a cream white, and his lapels were a sleek black color. His pockets and vest beneath were the same cream color with black accents, and he wore a black and white bowtie. Black pants that stopped right atop his white leather shoes, that I was certain had some kind of BT emblem on them, and his whole appearance winded me. I froze for a second, and I was embarrassed that the groom took the bride's breath away, but thankfully, Kat was there. She cleared her throat and got me moving down the aisle as she held my flowing train.

The walk seemed like a lifetime to make it to Vito, who stood poised and grinning like he was the happiest man in the world. As I made it to the altar, Vito removed my veil, and gasped. He blinked at me with a look of awe across his face and I did everything I could to keep from smiling so girlishly.

I'm happy, I thought as Vito and I recited our vows. *I am genuinely happy, I think. He makes me feel things I never knew existed, and I want to do the same for him.*

"Do you, Iyana Walters, take Vito Gerardo to be your lawfully wedded husband?"

I took a breath. "I do."

Vito smiled as the priest said, "I now pronounce you man and wife. You may kiss the bride."

Vito and I didn't spend much time together at the reception. We came in together, danced with each other, and with Emilia and Gio since they stood in as his parents, and then we ate. After cutting the cake, Vito sent me home, back to his apartment, where I got changed and relaxed. This was going to be my new home and I was no longer alone. From now on, Vito would always be here, and we'd be doing things together. While this was in no way a normal marriage, I couldn't shake the glee working its way up my spine and across my face as I changed to wait for Vito's return.

I didn't know how long he'd be gone since we had the venue until five in the morning, but I decided I'd stay up until midnight. During that time, I moved Challa into the guestroom, and a few of my things upstairs to Vito's place. He had already arranged for movers to come tomorrow, however, I wanted to grab a few things before then.

"Did you need some help?" Rion said as I stepped outside my place with a big vase.

"If you don't mind?" I shrugged.

He chuckled as he came over and retrieved the vase.

"Now, you've got to stand guard until I get back."

"Easy enough." I smiled.

As he turned to leave, he called over his shoulder, "Congratulations! I wish I could've seen you in your dress."

"I should've come down here, I hadn't even thought about it."

He stopped walking and faced me. "All that matters is the marriage, and that the boss found himself a good woman. I'm happy for you both."

"Thanks, Rion."

He nodded as he turned back and headed for the elevators. When I heard it ding, I twisted the handle and stepped inside. I'd been wanting to see Jewels, since I spoke with Alex to see how much they knew about each other or didn't know. From Jewels's behavior, it seemed like she really hadn't known anything about Alex.

As I stepped inside, I realized the entire place was messy and dark. There were papers all over the floor, and clothes, and overturned furniture. Ashtrays were broken, and on the back of the overturned couch, there were cigarette burns on it. The crunching beneath my slipper called my attention to the paper I was standing on.

"Pay to the order of J-N-J?" It was an invoice from the Morenos. They were paying someone by the name 'J-N-J' for a large order of molly. There were shipment dates, crate rates, and there was a printed name at the bottom, *Jefferson and Jewels.*

I gasped.

Brandon was working as more than a middleman. He wasn't taking clients for Gang Grizzly, he was taking them for himself. Which meant he was going to take a chance at creating his own gang or take over Gang Grizzly with his own fleet of clients.

"What are you doing?"

I looked up from the paper and found Jewels holding a burning cigarette. Silence fell and for a moment, I almost felt sorry for the disheveled woman. But the paper in my hand made me remember that she'd been working behind our backs all this time. Probably taking men from the brothel not as clients but using her private room to hold meetings and make deals.

I leaned down in a hurry and grabbed some more papers on the floor and sprinted out the room.

"Hey!" she screamed after me as she hurdled over a broken table. But she came down on a piece of glass and hollered out, allowing me to rip the door open and rush down the hall to the elevators. When they dinged, I rushed in past Rion and he said, "Hey, what's wrong?"

"Jewels is after me!"

He looked around and darted down the hall as I frantically hit the button for Vito's floor. The doors closed, and I could hear Jewels screaming and some kind of struggle. The sound began to muffle as the cart lifted me to the next floor.

Inside Vito's place, I read over the papers. Different invoices, all with the same *Jefferson & Jewels* emblem. Scrolling through the files on the computer, they matched with the bit of information I had from the sheets of paper I took from Jewels's place. My theory that these payments were going somewhere else was right, obviously, but I didn't realize that meant they weren't using our products. That must be where Brandon and Jewels came in. These legendary accounts were buying products from them, and their supply was a collection of stolen products from Gang Grizzly and BT, all stored in Brandon's warehouse.

"Brandon must be making payments to Grizzly from the money he's making off the Morenos if they're paying through him. If he has access to the shipments, then Brandon's getting free product without Grizzly knowing it." I paused as I jotted down some notes. "And he's selling it for a fortune and giving a portion of that to Grizzly under the guise of a payment from these legendary accounts."

I rocked back in my chair, twisting my pencil. "If we buy the company that's producing the products for Grizzly, we've got Brandon, Grizzly, and our legendary accounts back."

The door opened to the apartment, and Vito stepped inside. He took off his suit jacket, and I moved from my desk to greet him.

"Vito," I called.

He turned to me with a grin, tossing his jacket on the couch and grabbing me by my hips. "I couldn't wait to come home," he said as he leaned down and began kissing my neck.

"Vito, wait a second," I said, pushing him off.

He blinked. "We're married, Iyana, we can do this."

"I know, but I just made a discovery for BT that could help

us out."

"Iyana, it's our wedding night, we should be celebrating, not working."

I waved him off and headed back into my office. A moment later, he arrived in the doorway, unbuttoning his collar as he leaned against the post.

"I was looking over some files because I found some paperwork in Jewels's place."

"Why were you in there?"

I shrugged. "Anyways, I found that those five legendary accounts are all behind by more than three payments."

He shrugged too. "What's the discovery? We knew that."

"But we didn't realize we've been surviving without that money all this time because of new clients, investments, and our debtors paying us off. We've been bringing in more without them."

Vito began to remove his cufflinks. "That's good news." He straightened and took a step into my office, his footsteps echoing through his empty apartment. "But then we still have to worry about those five accounts going to Grizzly. He gets his hands on that kind of money, he can actually be a threat."

"Let him have them," I said.

Vito squinted. "Did you hear anything I just said? Money buys power."

"Exactly." I folded my arms, but he only sighed. "We let Grizzly have these guys, we own Grizzly."

"What are you talking about?"

I pushed from my chair and came around the desk to him.

"My first move as the leader of Bellen Tupp, is to buy the suppliers of these legendary accounts. Right now, they're actually paying Brandon and Jewels." I passed him one of the invoices from Jewels's place and he looked it over as I explained.

"They're taking product from Grizzly's shipments and reselling them. They're giving a portion of that money to Grizzly and pocketing the rest. If we cut them off, we've got everyone."

He nodded. "But they're pocketing all the money from the legendary accounts and giving the money they've been soliciting from my other accounts to Grizzly."

"What do you mean?"

"Gio and Emilia and a few of my other clients were visited by Brandon to collect payments early. Those payments are probably the ones being used to keep Grizzly off their backs."

"Either way," I nodded, "if we find the supplier and buy them out, we technically own Gang Grizzly, J-N-J, and we get all our accounts back."

Vito chuckled. "It sounds easier than it'll be. Considering we'll have to get people to talk."

"We still have Alex to consider if all else fails," I suggested weakly.

"We now have Jewels, too. When she realizes what's missing, she might turn on Brandon if we can give her information about Alex."

"Good." I smiled widely. "Then I'll have Leo and Kat on the investigation."

Vito stood silent for a moment before he surrendered to another chuckle. "Iyana Gerardo, Ana Ortega, you are the smartest woman in the entire world." He took a step toward me and wrapped his arms around my waist. I giggled foolishly in his arms, elated that my first move as the head of BT was actually a good one. When my smile began to wither, Vito leaned down to kiss me, but I shrank away.

"I'm sorry," I said, stepping from his embrace, "I just—"

"It's late," he shrugged, "I'm going to bed."

"Alright." I clasped my hands together, regretful that I'd rejected him. "I'll just head to my place."

Vito stopped in my doorway and turned around. "We're married now, you can sleep here. I'll sleep on the couch if it makes you feel any better."

"Right," I said slowly.

"Most newlyweds don't forget they're married on their wedding night or choose to work."

"I know, it's just," I paused because I didn't mean to work, and I wasn't sure how to tell Vito I was apprehensive about sex. I had my reasons, of course; the first was because I didn't know if we loved each other, and I wanted to share my first time with someone I loved. The second was that I was a virgin. I didn't know how well I'd perform since Vito wasn't a virgin. But I had to pick a reason as he waited for an answer. So I picked the one I thought would be less embarrassing and would get me to my apartment the quickest.

I took a deep breath and forced myself to blurt out, "I'm a virgin!"

Vito flinched when I yelled but recovered quickly. He grabbed his chest and sighed. "I'm glad that's the problem. Well, it isn't a *problem*, but it is a relief."

I scratched my head. "Relief?"

"I thought you were going to tell me that you really didn't like me. You really were in this for BT only."

"That's the thing," I turned and slumped against my desk, "I do like you, Vito, and I want to share myself with you. I just feel like I'll be a disappointing wife. Sexually, at least."

Vito sighed and came and leaned against the desk beside me. He only looked down at my feet, although, I could tell from the faint red tint on his ears that this conversation was equally as embarrassing for him.

"Iyana, that doesn't matter to me." He paused, gripping the table nervously. "I can't pinpoint a time when my feelings for you changed, and I know you think it all changed when you saved me at the store. But something happened before then, *way* before then, that changed me and everything about me. I just don't want to say I've been in love with you since I met you, but I think it might be true."

"What happened?"

"It was your second night here, I think, and you fell asleep in my office. I didn't know right away that you were asleep until I got closer to you." He swallowed and suddenly I was wondering if this was a confession or something else. "There were tears on your cheeks. You were crying in your sleep. I wondered how someone could be so hurt, so shattered, that even when they were supposed to be resting, supposed to be disappearing into a world where they couldn't remember the present, that they were still crying. They were still experiencing that hurt." Silence washed over us once again, before Vito could bring himself to speak once more.

"You were so fragile, I thought I'd broken you. To know that I was the reason for those tears that night, it changed me." He took a breath. "But then you started getting stronger, and every day it got harder to breathe around you. My mind was always wandering and spending every day with you was something I began to look forward to." He laughed. "When you work, you wrinkle your nose when something's not right."

I immediately covered my nose as he went on.

"You toy with your fingers when you're bored. And sometimes, you gaze out the window, and I imagine you're longing to be where you used to be. I loved watching you, protecting you, and somewhere along the line, I realized I was watching and protecting you because I loved you."

I sat still beside him. I didn't know that Vito felt something real for me. That all this time, I've meant more to him than I knew.

I shook my head, trying to fight the tears as Vito said, "I was planning to ask you to marry me anyway, just under different circumstances. I wanted you to get out of BT, and for my men to follow you wherever you went. So that one day, when I walked away from here, I could find you and make up for lost time. I could tell you all the things I loved about you. Unfortunately, business is business."

"I would've waited," I said quietly. "I would've waited for

you in the hopes that you'd come find me one day. I want to be here because you're here. I don't want to be anywhere without you." I paused, shakily reaching for his hand curled over the edge of the desk. Our fingers interlocked and Vito looked at me, I'd never seen him like this before. He wasn't bewildered, he wasn't emotional. He was calm, he was in love, and I was the one he was in love with. "Cortez," I said quietly. Shock zipped across his face as I used his real name. But it only lasted a moment before melting away as I told him, "I love you too."

25

Dirty Decisions

"You might want to slow down," the bartender said.

"Just hit me again," I snapped. "I know my limit."

She shrugged as she took my glass and walked away. Tonight was the worst night of my life. Vito was marrying Iyana, and I'd wasted the two weeks Grizzly gave me chasing accounts that fell through with no signs of the Abletons.

The bartender returned with a shot of liquor, and I took it from her before she could even slide it to me. I guzzled it down, and slammed the glass onto the counter, followed by two, one-hundred-dollar bills.

The room swayed as I made my way through the dance floor. A woman grabbed me and tried to dance, but I shoved her so hard to the floor, the crowd around us gasped.

"What is wrong with you?" A dark-skinned woman leaned

down to help her friend, and I shook my head, shoving my way through the crowd. Rushing outside, I vomited all over the icy parking lot. The day was ending and tomorrow I'd have to report to Grizzly with no information about the Abletons, with no information about anything.

Jewels had gotten me meetings, but everyone was so interested in Vito's marriage, they weren't looking to do business with a smaller gang. All the work I've put in was about to amount to nothing. What would I tell Jewels? How would I take care of Alex?

Getting off my knees, I crossed the lot to my truck and climbed inside. I'd always told Jewels I'd make her my wife once I took over Gang Grizzly. We were going to change the name to J-N-J, had even convinced a few of our clients that our gang was slowly coming together. Now, I was about to lose access to Grizzly, possibly even lose my life.

I opened my phone to call Jewels, and when I saw Alex and BJ's picture, my heart cracked. Maybe it was time I gave up this life and just started over with them. We could get away from New York, go somewhere even Vito couldn't reach us. It would be easier that way, simpler.

Shakily, I dialed Alex's number and listened to the ringing.

"Hello?" she said tiredly.

"Alex, baby?"

"What's wrong?" Her voice was more alert now. "Is everything alright?"

"Yeah." I cleared my throat. "Yeah, I just..." I paused. "I need to tell you something."

Silence.

"It can't wait until the morning?"

"Let's move," I said abruptly.

"Move? BJ just started school, and I'm due soon. We can't just move, Brandon."

"What about that little spot," I said, "the one in Hawaii that you tried to get me to move to when we first got married."

She laughed tiredly into the phone. Alex and I had become so distant, I don't know how she stayed with me. But listening to her laugh, listening to her voice, the only thing that brought me clarity … I began to regret my entire life. I hated myself for what I'd put her through. Now it was going up in flames and I wanted to run away to save her.

"I remember," she said, calling my attention back to her. "I wanted to live off grid in Hawaii and visit the beach every day."

"Yeah," I almost choked, "that was it."

I could hear her shifting in the bed. "Well, maybe after the baby is born, we can buy some land and settle there. It'll be nice for the kids, I think, growing up on a beach." I heaved a large sniffle as I toppled over onto the steering wheel.

"Brandon, are you alright?"

"I'm sorry," I said in a whisper.

"What happened?" She was quiet for a moment. "Was it your job?"

"Yeah, my job. I think they're going to let me go."

"What happened?"

"It's a long story." I sighed. "Can you be awake when I get

home?"

"Yes," she said. "I'll put on some coffee for you."

"Alex," I called, clutching the phone.

"Yes?"

"I love you."

Silence.

"You're scaring me," she said.

"I'm sorry." I took a breath. "I just wanted to tell you that."

"Well, come home already. I'm getting up now."

"Ok, bye."

"Bye," she said.

I leaned back in my chair and sighed. Getting Alex involved was a bad move, but I had no one else. Jewels wouldn't understand, Grizzly was going to kill me, and Vito was gallivanting off with his new wife. Not that he would help me anyway.

I started my truck and backed out the parking lot. Cruising down the quiet street, I tried to put together a way to tell Alex the truth. I didn't even know if she would believe me, but I knew she was going to want a reason for abruptly wanting to leave, and for thinking I was going to get fired.

I had nothing but the truth, although I wished for another lie. Telling Alex the truth meant telling her about Jewels, and she might not forgive me for that. I loved Alex, but somewhere in my heart, I know I loved Jewels too. She was the mother of my son, the only woman, the only person, to ever genuinely like me and care about me as a gang member. If I told Alex the truth, I'd be turning on Jewels, and I didn't know if I could do that to her.

Alex always overshadowed Jewels, but there have been times when thoughts of running away with Jewels was the only thing that kept me from losing my mind. Alex was pure, but Jewels was sullied like me. We'd done so much together; it seemed wrong to turn on her for a woman who didn't even know the truth. But I loved Alex more than I could bear. If I ran away with Jewels, Alex would have nothing. But if I ran away with Alex, Jewels would be alright.

As I pulled to a stop at a red a light, I spotted Gio's Diner. Emilia was getting out the car, and so were Gio and Gio Jr. They were all dressed nicely, like they'd been somewhere fancy. Then it hit me, they'd gone to Vito's wedding, and that struck a nerve. Everyone went to his wedding, but that wedding was destroying all my plans. That wedding was taking everything from me, and now was my chance to take something from Vito.

He owed me. He owed me for forcing me to turn on him. If he hadn't stepped up, I could've been head of BT without involving Alex or even Jewels to a certain extent. I could feel the rage burning in my chest, could feel all the fear of tomorrow churning in my stomach and I couldn't take it.

I slammed my foot on the gas and sped off through the red light. I swerved around a turning car as it honked at me, and I mounted the curb. Squeezing the steering wheel, I pressed down harder on the gas as I swerved into Gio's parking lot and rammed my truck into their car.

"Junior!" Emilia cried.

I backed up once more and, in my rage, I rammed the truck forward again, hoping to crush them. To leave absolutely nothing behind. I wanted to take something from Vito the way he'd taken everything from me. The way I'd been left with absolutely nothing.

This time, as I hit the gas, I took the car through the building. Emilia and Gio screeched as I rammed into them, but the sound of my truck crashing through the restaurant silenced them both. The sudden quiet was loud and painful, forcing me to realize what I'd done. But I didn't want to dwell on it.

Reversing once more, I drove off onto the street, and took the side streets home.

When I pulled up to the house, I hopped out the car and hollered for Alex.

"Lex! Get out here!"

She came bursting from the front door in her housecoat. She turned on the porch light and rushed down the stairs, but she stopped when she saw the truck.

Covering her mouth, she said, "What have you done?"

"I…" I faltered, "I hit a deer."

"There are no deer around here."

"I don't know what I hit." I shook my head. "I just need your help getting the truck clean. Get the hose from the back and don't ask any more questions."

"No." She shook her head and backed away. "I am not going to help with this."

I'd had enough. I was tired. I'd lost everything, and I came all the way back for her. I thought Alex was different. I thought

I was making the right decision to run away with her, but I was wrong.

Jewels was the one for me. This proved it. Jewels would've helped without hesitation. I turned on her, but for what? I wanted to get in the car and go get Jewels, but I couldn't, not like this.

But what if I'm wrong? What if Jewels wouldn't help me, either? I'm here now, I've only got a little time before someone who saw me crashing into Gio's Diner found me, or before Grizzly emerged from his den to find me. I needed to be out of here, and since Alex was here, I was taking her with me.

I grinded my teeth and yelled, "You don't love me anymore!"

She shook her head, glancing between the truck and me.

"Then prove it and help me right now. I need you, Alex."

"No," she said again. "I can't do this. You need to leave." She sniffled. "You are putting me and your children in danger with this! Leave before whatever you're running from finds you."

"Excuse me? Alex, get down here and help me!"

"No!" she snapped. "I can't keep doing this! I can't stand the lies!"

My legs felt like lightning struck them as I stormed to her in seconds. I snatched her by the wrist and dragged her behind me. "You are going to help me, and we are leaving!"

"No!" she screamed as she twisted and jerked, but it was no use.

I gripped her tightly before flinging her to the ground in

front of the truck. Slowly, she lifted her head, and was face to face with blood and debris. She began to gag. Slapping a hand over her mouth, she tried to get to her feet, but I snatched her by the hair and shoved her face into the ground.

"You gonna vomit? You're going to do it right here," I said in her ear.

She began to sob and belch at the same time as she cradled her belly, but I didn't care. I was beyond caring at this point. I'd just murdered an entire family, there wasn't any room for sympathy.

My lips peeled back into a snarl as I growled out an ultimatum, "Help me, or we're both going to die."

26

Holding Your Breath

The wedding went on all night, but I had to retire at two. When I left, Logan was still on the dancefloor with some girl he'd been dancing with all night. Kat left right after pictures, before the reception even started, and Leo only stayed until the cake was cut. Both returned to the Tower, and both greeted me in their normal suits and ties as I entered. Kat's hair had returned to its bun, and Leo's was free of the product he'd used to keep it sleek during the wedding.

"How was the party, Hardy?" Leo asked as I came to the front desk.

"It was a lot of fun," I said, giving Leo a knowing look. He nodded, but Kat only rolled her eyes.

"Wish I could've stayed," Leo agonized.

Kat looked back at her screen, and I said, "You would've

had a lot of fun. Probably more than standing here with Kat."

She didn't budge.

"Probably," Leo muttered through a low chuckle.

"Leo," she turned and handed him a flashlight, "you're on patrol tonight."

Defeated, he took the flashlight and quietly dressed for the heavy snow falling outdoors before leaving us alone. Kat and I had been talking more frequently since we'd had that lunch together. But she was being such a stickler about me seeing her, I didn't know what we were, if we were even anything more than friends.

"Did you need something, Hardy?" she asked, looking up from her screen.

"Yeah, you could come to my place, and—"

"Haven't you had enough? There's already been one girl down your pants, despite the venue, I don't think you need another."

"You sound jealous."

"And you sound desperate," she fired back.

I nodded, backing away as she returned to her screen. I took the elevator to Iyana's floor as I mulled over whether or not sex with a woman I couldn't even remember meant I was desperate. What was I even desperate for? I didn't need to ask that. I'd been vying for Jewels's attention since that black tie event. She's completely shut me out, and I haven't been able to get her to talk to me, let alone see me. The car ride home after that event was silent. Dragging her back to her apartment hadn't been a quiet event, but she'd only screamed threats at

Iyana, so technically we still didn't talk.

I sighed as I stepped off the elevator. Coming down the hall to Iyana's place, I noticed Jewels's door was cracked. My heart nearly skipped a beat as I rushed over to it and pushed it open. The lights were dimmed and there were papers and garbage everywhere. Some furniture had been turned over. As I crept further inside, I saw someone sitting on the couch.

I jumped back and stood still, trying to listen, but there was no sound coming from the person, no movement, nothing. I stepped out again and peered around at the couch. The person was sitting perfectly still. Arms spread over the top; the figure looked like a man. Something felt off, and I reached for my gun. Whipping it out, I took painfully slow steps over to the couch, but when I came around, I gasped so hard I began to choke.

Rion had a bullet in his head. He was leaning back into the cushions like he'd been relaxing when he was shot. He never expected it. *In fact, he was expecting something else*, I noted as I stared at his pants around his ankles. I glanced around for his gun, before realizing that his killer used his own weapon. If a gunshot had gone off, no matter if Iyana and Vito were next door or upstairs, they would've heard it. But Rion always carried a silencer attached to his gun, so whoever shot him took his weapon from him first. Whoever shot him had distracted him…

"Jewels," I whispered.

I jogged through her place and when I didn't find her, I rushed to the elevator and headed to the front desk.

"Kat! Kat!" I called as I rounded the corner.

"What?"

"Rion," I panted, "he's been shot, and I think Jewels did it."

"What?" She erupted from her chair and came around the desk. "Is he still alive? Where is she?"

"I don't know, but Rion's dead. It looked like they were in the middle of something." I shrugged.

She shook her head. "Alright, I'm going to find Jewels. You get a team together to get his body out of here."

"Let me go find her, I can talk her down before you can."

She hesitated but gave in. "Fine but only apprehend her—don't hurt her."

"And Vito? What do we tell him?"

"Nothing until we've caught her. Now go."

I jogged off down the hall, searching for where Jewels might be. I checked the park first, she sometimes liked to go there to clear her head, but she wasn't there. I went to Logan's place and got inside. He still wasn't home, and she wasn't there either. They hadn't done a good job at hiding their relationship, and it was driving me crazy. But it was easier to pretend like it wasn't happening than to face reality.

I left his apartment and went to the only other place she might go, the brothel room. I stood at the purple door which was cracked open. At this hour, there was usually no one there, everyone was at work. Taking a deep breath, I pushed the door open and hoped I wouldn't find another dead body.

"Jewels?" I called meekly.

There was no reply.

"Jewels?" I called again as I approached the bathing room. There was light pouring from there, and when I stepped inside, I found Jewels rinsing her hair at a tub.

"Jewels," I said, kneeling beside her.

She jumped when I pressed my hand to her back, spilling water and hair dye all over the floor. "Hardy?"

"What's going on? We found Rion; they're coming for you, Jewels. So you better tell me something or I can't help you."

"I don't need your help," she said as she took her gloves off. She stood to her feet and rushed around the room, ripping her soggy shirt from her body to swap it for a fresh one from her duffle bag.

"Where are you going?" I said behind her. "Why did you kill Rion?"

"I'm leaving, Hardy."

"And going where?"

"Anywhere. But I've got to figure out my own life."

I watched her force her feet into socks as I said, "Take me with you. I'll go wherever you go. I'll get another job. I'll take care of us." I moved to wrap my arms around her, but she forced me away.

"Stop it, Hardy. You're not going."

"Why not? Jewels, I love you."

She stiffened, turning to face me with tears in her eyes. "I don't love you, Hardy. You made me feel good, made me feel vibrant."

"You don't mean that," I said.

"I do. I needed you when I was down, and it was wrong to use you, but I don't love you."

"That's not true!" I barked.

"Yes, it is! I love Brandon! He's the father of my son! I have to go find him, and we're going to run away together. We're going to get away from you, and Vito, and Iyana, and all of BT and New York. We're going to leave, and no one's going to find us." She whirled away but I grabbed her by the arm.

"You don't mean that," I said shakily. My heart was racing hard, and my chest was tightening. How could she love anyone but me? I've never loved another woman more than her.

"Jewels, please, I love you," I pleaded.

"You love having sex with me, Hardy, but you don't love me. And I don't love you."

She tried to pull her arm from me, but I saw red, and my grip tightened. When she screamed, it only infuriated me more because I would never hurt her, but all along she's been hurting me. She deserved whatever pain she was feeling.

"You've never meant anything you've said to me. Has it all been a lie?"

"Yes!" she bellowed. "Everything between us has just been one disgusting lie! You're a child, Hardy!"

"No." I shook my head as tears blurred my eyes. "No, you don't mean that!"

She ripped free from me and ran to her bag. Fumbling through it, she tried to pull her gun out, but I tackled her without thinking. In seconds, she was beneath me on the floor, scrambling to get free. But I overpowered her as my mind numbed and my thoughts went blank. I couldn't think, I could only move.

My hands ripped at her shirt, exposing her breasts. "I'm going to prove you love me," I growled.

"Stop it!" she screamed.

I forced my mouth over hers, kissing her relentlessly, but she fought me off.

"Stop it, Hardy!"

Her words were muffled against my lips. I could see her fighting against me, I could see her struggling. But the anger surging through me suddenly cooled into an electric jolt of ecstasy, like the rage, the hurt, and the frustration had finally been set free. All three came together as one the moment I wrapped my hands around her throat. All the pain she caused me, I wanted her to feel it too. I wanted her to suffer by my hands as I'd suffered at hers.

She continued to thrash beneath me, but the more she struggled, the harder I squeezed, until she wasn't thrashing anymore. But even then, I couldn't take my hands from around her neck.

Tears fell from my eyes to her cheeks, and something inside me broke as I whispered, "Please, don't leave me."

27

Blood Has Been Spilled

Iyana laid in bed with her head on my chest as I stared up at the ceiling. I wasn't tired since I'd been staying up later these past two weeks to make sure she had the wedding she wanted. Deals, promises, business exchanges ... in the morning, our lives would become hectic. We'd be overwhelmed with inquiries, having Iyana meet with some of our bigger clients, we'd even be losing some business. But for now, we needed to rest.

"Vito!" Just as I'd began to drift off, a voice pierced through the silence and my eyes shot open. "Vito!"

I shook Iyana, and she drowsily lifted her head.

"Roll over," I told her.

She agreed sleepily and turned over in bed and I crept out of it.

"Where are you going?" Iyana asked.

"Just stay in bed." I leaned over and kissed her head after I pulled my clothes on. I barged out the bedroom to find Hardy standing in the middle of the living room, trembling.

"What's wrong?" I asked.

"It's Jewels," he choked. His eyes were bulging—I'd never seen him this scared before. He was even more frightened than when he'd first arrived here as ransom.

"What's wrong with her?"

"I killed her."

A rigid moment passed with neither of us speaking. Hardy just stood there trembling while I tried to make sense of things.

I took a deep breath and finally said, "Where is she?"

"In the brothel room."

I nodded. "Ok, here's what you're going to do—"

"Vito?" Iyana called sleepily.

I turned around to find her standing in my shirt, pushing her hair from her face.

"Go back to bed," I said.

"Why? What's going on? I can help."

"All I need is for you to get some rest. We've got a busy morning, alright? Please, Ana, go back to bed."

She studied me, and then glanced over at Hardy. I know she wanted to press the issue but, mercifully, she nodded and went back to the bedroom.

"Vito!" Kat's voice came from behind the door.

I looked at Hardy, but there wasn't much else I was going

to get from him. I left him and moved to the door.

"What is it?" I asked as I held the door open.

"Something's happened," she started. "Jewels killed Rion, but I just found Jewels's dead body in the brothel room. Someone killed her, but I don't know who."

I stepped to the side and cracked the door open a little wider. Her eyes widened and then shrank.

"What do you want to do?" she asked.

I shook my head. "I don't know yet. For now, take both Rion's and Jewels's bodies to the cellar and put them in the freezer."

"Are you planning on using them?"

"I might," I said, "but I don't know yet. And I still need to figure out what to do with Hardy."

"Let me talk to him. I'll send Leo to take care of the bodies. You go rest for now. God knows we'll need you rested for the morning."

"Fine." I turned and called for Hardy. "Come over here, Kat's going to take care of everything."

Reluctantly, he came to the door, but he never lifted his eyes to see her or me.

"Come on." She took his hand and led him down the hall in silence. I closed the door, leaning my head against it.

"One good day," I whispered to myself.

"Vito."

I kept my head on the door and my eyes closed as I said, "Iyana ... Rion and Jewels are dead."

"Oh my goodness. What happened?"

"I'm not sure," I confessed. I didn't know if I should tell her about Hardy, or if I should keep things quiet, but Iyana's next words shocked me.

"Hardy killed her, didn't he?"

"Yeah," I said flatly.

"He found out she didn't love him." She paused. "He's so young, he thought they were in love."

"Well…" I turned to face her; she was still in my shirt as she hugged herself. "We've got to get some rest. I'll have to figure out how to handle this in the—" the telephone rang, making Iyana flinch. No one called the Tower; my clients only used my personal number. There was only one person alive who knew the number to the Tower, and as I picked up the phone, the caller was exactly who I expected.

"Cortez, sorry to call this late."

"Dad, what is it?"

Iyana came over to the phone and I leaned over for her to hear. "It's Emilia. She tried your personal line, but she said it was off, so she called me."

"Emilia? Why did she call?"

There was a pit opening in my stomach, like a darkness churning and spewing anxiety and bitterness into my entire body.

"She said there was an accident. Someone drove off the road and crashed into their diner."

"What? Is everyone alright?" He was quiet for a moment too long. Beside me, I saw Iyana cover her mouth.

"Gio Jr. is in critical condition, they don't think he'll make it through the next hour. Gio Sr. didn't make it."

Iyana nearly collapsed, and I dropped the phone to catch her. Shakily, she breathed, and I could hear my father calling for me on the other end. Lifting Iyana, I carried her to the couch and set her there before returning to the phone.

"Hello?"

"What just happened?" Dad asked. I glanced over at Iyana on the couch, she had curled up and was crying into a pillow.

"It was Iyana, she almost passed out."

"What? Why would you let her know?"

"She was going to find out anyway."

"Vito, are you thinking with your head? I know she's the leader of BT but there are still things you cannot let her handle."

"I know," I said, raking a hand over my hair.

"I'm coming out there in the morning."

"What? No," I said sternly.

"Yes, and that's final."

"Dad if you come out here right now, the day after my wedding, everyone will think BT just fell apart because of Iyana. People will think we're weak. Do not come here and ruin everything I've built from your ashes."

My father didn't speak for a while, giving me a moment to let things sink in that I didn't want to. I wanted to believe it was some freak accident that took Gio Sr. and in any moment, Gio Jr., but I was afraid it wasn't.

Gio was like a father to me. Since I couldn't speak with my father, he really stepped up and took care of me. Gio and

Emilia were my gang affiliated parents, how could it have come to this? Who would want to hurt them? Especially after tonight.

I showed the world that I was not alone. I showed them that the people closest to me were untouchable, and yet, two of those people are now dead. Something wasn't right. And fear was wrapping her thin arms around me. Because I told the world who was off limits, yet I was still challenged. Did that mean BT already looked weak? How much danger was Iyana actually in?

"Dad?" I called into the silence, trying to fight the panic swelling in my chest.

"Yeah?"

"Gio and Emilia stood in as my parents today at the wedding. Gio Jr. was like the brother I never had. We took family pictures. So why? Why would someone do this?"

He sighed. "If it wasn't an accident—"

"It wasn't," I snapped.

He cleared his throat. "Then someone's trying to send you a message. They're trying to break up your happy family. They want to ruin you. Don't let them do it, Vito."

My dad only used my leader name when he was serious—when he needed to stop being my father to remind me that he was the leader of BT before me. Despite my father's mess-ups in his last few years, and no matter how much work I've done to surpass him, I will only be the Prince of the Apple. My father will always be the reigning king.

"Who would do something like this?"

"It's got to be Grizzly."

"But why? He knows the rules. I hadn't made my move yet."

"You hadn't moved at all, had you? You were trying to call it quits."

"We don't need a gang war. I was just trying to drag it out until it fizzled into nothing."

"By not retaliating? Vito, come on. You know Grizzly's antsy."

"But that works in our favor now. They jumped the gun, now we can do what we want."

"Now you have to kill someone, and I know you don't want to. You have to retaliate, Vito, or your clients will think you're not a good leader. They'll never believe that you'll protect them. They're all waiting for your move. You just made this war public. Now you'll have to perform."

I gritted my teeth, feeling the seething anger burn in my clenched fist. "What do I do?"

"You make a move. A good one. Put his back against the wall, do something outlandish. This war isn't political anymore." He paused, and sickness twisted in my stomach. "There will be bloodshed."

"Alright," I said weakly.

He was right. My plan had backfired and opened a door to chaos, the one door I was trying so hard to keep closed. Everything I'd done to keep BT away from bloodshed was meaningless. Keeping Iyana away was meaningless because now there was unbearable responsibility on her shoulders.

People know that I'm not weak, but they know nothing about her.

"She'll have to prove herself... Won't she?" I asked flatly.

The silence that followed made me hunch over, gripping the small table the phone was sitting on.

"Yes," my father answered calmly. "Iyana will have to prove that BT is worth investing in and can still be trusted despite all that's happened. She will have to wear the crown, Vito. Do you understand?"

An uncontrollable war was brewing—no—it was *storming* around us, with Iyana at the center. As the new leader of BT, she will have to make all the decisions. She will have to bear the Cross I've loathed all this time. She will become the monster I have feared, and there's nothing I can do to protect her.

My father asked me again, "Do you understand, Vito?"

Shakily, I took a breath. "Yes, I understand."

Finish the series…

The Bite of the Alpha
(Winter 2022)

More books by A. Bean & TRC Publishing!

Christian Fantasy
The End of the World series
The Scribe
Cross Academy series

Christian Science Fiction
I AM MAN series

Christian Romance
The Living Water
Withered Rose Trilogy
Fractured Diamond

Christian Children's Fiction
Too Young

ACKNOWLEDGEMENTS

Jesus is the Christ, Son of the Living God. He is the One who gave me the idea and enabled me to write this story, thank you.

My mother's love for action and thrillers and my inability to skip a chance on a little drama has made The Woof Pack: The Beta Rises, what it is today.

Sign up for my [monthly newsletter](#) to stay updated on new releases, sales, and updates! See you soon.

The Rebel Christian Publishing

We are an independent Christian publishing company focused on fantasy, science fiction, and romantic reads. Visit therebelchristian.com to check out our books!

  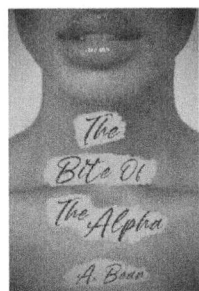

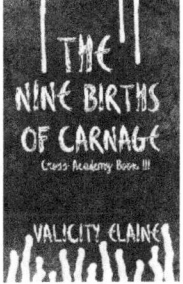

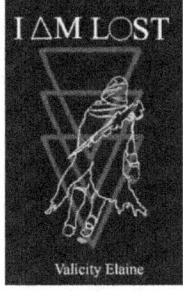
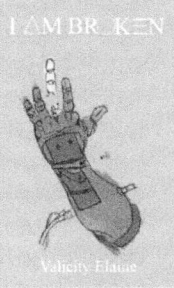
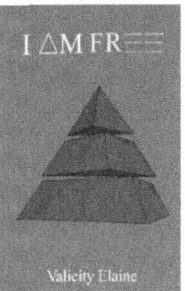
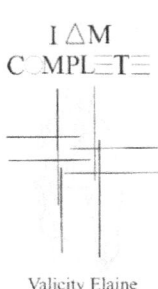

Made in United States
North Haven, CT
18 January 2025

64579470R00157